I0575226

IN THE REEDS

By Tim Maddox
First Published December 12, 2024

The works within are fictional, save for the two exceptions detailed below. Any resemblance to reality should be considered inspirational or purely coincidental.

"My Life, No?" is autobiographical, up until the final four paragraphs.

"Autumnal Fire" is my personal reflection on my life during the autumn of 2020 and the COVID lockdowns up to that point in time (October 2020).

If you would like to participate in the Reedsy weekly prompts or read stories from others who have, you can find them at: blog.reedsy.com/creative-writing-prompts

Cover design: Tim Maddox via Canva

Author website:
www.tim-maddox-books.square.site

ISBNs: 979-8-9921954-0-8 (paperback)
         979-8-9921954-1-5 (E-book)

Table of Contents:

Foreword

The Completed Stories:

The Unfinished Tales:

Afterword

FOREWORD

Firstly, I want to thank you for choosing to read this collection. Picking up any anthology collection is a gamble, and I hope that I make good on that gamble.

The stories within *In The Reeds* all come from a writing prompt for Reedsy.com's weekly writing contests. Five prompts would be released every Friday, and you had until the next Friday to submit a 1,000-to-3,000-word story. I participated in these contests for just shy of a year, from February 2020 to January of 2021.

This collection includes the 11 stories that were submitted within the week deadline, in order of the contests they were submitted for, as well as three other tales that I started, but didn't quite finish in time. These three would have been between "My Life, No?" and "Peregrine" if originally completed.

To be up front, the 11 completed stories have received some editing from their 2020-2021 forms. All the completed originals can still be found on Reedsy's writing prompt website if you wish to compare.

Now, the title *In The Reeds* isn't simply a pun towards the origin point of these stories. The only throughline among them is that I wrote them from one of that week's prompts.

For example, you will find first person contemporary narratives in "My Life, No?", "Autumnal Fire", and the completely fictional "The Remembered Past", but they surround a science fiction wingsuit chase in "Peregrine" that got a spy-thriller prelude with "Blackout" a few contests later, along with "Of Ladies and Tigers", where I flipped the perspective on the classic short story "The Lady, or the Tiger?", written by Frank R. Stockton all the way back in 1882.

"For Honor and Blood", where a mercenary captain asks his commanders to follow him on one last adventure to save his homeland, is the only story in the collection that was inspired by and part of a story I've been working on. That week's prompt brought a new scene to mind, and I used that for the contest.

In another fantasy setting, "Jealous Flames" shows the moment where a former ally turns up to enact revenge for being on the losing end of a love triangle.

"Into the Faerie Realm", where a king's huntsman chases a faerie into her hidden realm, is the short story which I have had the hardest time with. I wrote it in one day, having discovered Reedsy that afternoon and the deadline being in the evening. It is therefore the first story I ever submitted, but I've always wished I hadn't rushed it.

The two "Blizzard" tales that mark the end of the completed stories of this collection were written and submitted for two different prompts for the same weekly contest. They currently stand as the last short stories I wrote for the contests as my life took a turn shortly after.

As to the three unfinished tales, I chose the ones that were nearest completion from the stories that weren't finished in the week deadline, either because I couldn't land the ending or couldn't find a way to knit the middle together. Incidentally, all three also have their lead finding themselves in a new world.

"A Father's Legacy" is loosely part of the interconnected series of realms introduced in "Into the Faerie Realm", with Will's father having entered Andulan's realm and Will learning that the stories were real.

"Through the Wormhole" tells the tale of Wolfgang discovering the wormhole that his father has been chasing, but curiosity gets the better of him and he finds a magical world on the other side.

"Survival Games" finds our hero Luke having fallen asleep on his way home from a college beach trip and waking up in a forest. He quickly discovers two groups of people, and then a battle begins.

Thank you for reading through this quick summation of what lies in the pages beyond. If any of these tales do catch your eye or you have any feedback, feel free to reach out and let me know. I'm always looking to improve my craft.

Enjoy.

THE COMPLETED

STORIES

"INTO THE FAERIE REALM"

Contest #30: Write a story in which someone finds a secret passageway.

"Halt!" Matthias yelled at the fleeing figure.

It was his responsibility as one of King Thaddeus' huntsmen to protect the forests from poachers. Matthais had originally spotted the young woman getting a drink from the stream. She had long blonde hair, a yellow tunic that complemented her lithe form, and she carried a bow. When she had spotted him, she had fled.

True, he had approached her with his bow drawn, but he couldn't be too cautious. A pretty girl was a pretty girl, but a poacher was a poacher.

He knew this part of the forests like the back of his hand. Meanwhile, she appeared to be running as though she was confused. She must be new to the trade, or desperate. It had been a difficult winter after all, and the fields were only just being plowed.

Matthias initially made great gains as they weaved through his favorite terrain, but the deeper they went into the forest, the less those gains were.

Up ahead he could see the forest floor turning blue. The bluebells were in bloom, meaning that they were nearing the Ancient Woods. It was the setting of old myths about elves and faeries and other magical creatures, of wars and the heroes of old. Catwal the Brave, Andulan the Builder, King Thaddeus the Lawgiver. Bards sang those tales at every festival.

Whether because of these myths or not, there were strict laws about entering the Woods' boundaries. He himself had only entered a handful of times because of the reverence of the place, and never without first informing the king and going through the rituals.

Yet she flew past the boundary without hesitation.

Now she had broken more laws than just poaching.

Matthias continued to pursue her, his oath to protect the land overcoming his hesitance. Each step deeper she ran with more confidence, and each step made him angrier. For a poacher to make a haven in such a place, one that both kings and priests had declared sacred, was appalling.

The chase continued for some time. Matthias was young and known for his endurance, but she was keeping a pace that was starting to tax him. He could try to draw his bow and stop her with an arrow, but the idea was quickly brushed aside. A wounded and cornered animal was the most dangerous.

In the distance, he heard the sound of falling water. She was heading right for it.

The bluebells were growing scattered now as new flowers took their place. Matthias took a quick glance at them. They were yellow like her tunic and tipped with a pink color. He had never seen these before.

How far is her hideout?

When he looked up from the flowers, the young woman had changed her course, ducking behind a hedge that had just appeared. Matthias hurried to the hedge and rounded it. He was greeted by a pool of still water, a stream flowing from one end and a waterfall ten feet tall on the other. It puzzled him how the water could be still with such features.

He stared at it for a few moments, thinking of how it reminded him of the old bardic tales. Then he shook his head and returned to his quarry.

There was no longer any sign of the girl. That in itself was frustrating, but not disheartening. He was one of the king's best hunters. The chase may have ended, but the hunt was now afoot.

His eyes glanced at the ground. There he could easily make out her footsteps, though they were not as prominent as he would have expected. She was exceedingly light on her feet. He followed the footsteps to the side of the waterfall, the terrain switching from flowered grass to muddy shore and finally to bare rock. If not for the tracks of mud he might have lost her trail.

Then it just simply vanished.

Before him was a solid wall of stone beside the waterfall. No sign of handholds, no muddy prints, nothing.

He surveyed either side of the trail. Nothing.

Where did she go?!

Matthias knew that she couldn't have just vanished. He strained his eyes to find any clues. Then he backtracked her trail, looking for anything out of the ordinary.

Still nothing.

Now he was bewildered. That was the only word Matthias could think of. Yet there had to be an answer, and it had to be related to the wall. He turned back and walked over to it.

When the stone wall was before him again, he stroked his chin. Whatever she had done, it had to have been done quickly with how close he had been behind her.

His eyes still down, he looked to the young woman's last steps. They showed no telltale signs of exerting a force to jump. Maybe a small leap forward, but nothing like she'd need to reach the waterfall.

Matthais looked back along the trail. She had never wavered in her heading.

Certain that this spot held significance, Matthias studied the wall. There was still nothing that stood out to him, but he knew that the clue was staring right at him. In the back of his mind, he worried about how far away the young woman was while he stood here. It was a worry that would cloud his judgement if he focused on it, so he ignored it as best he could.

Thinking of her did give him a new idea though. One inspired by the bardic tales that the place invoked. He set his feet over her footsteps, then lowered himself to roughly her height. His eyes danced slowly across the surface, until at long last a set of shadows caught his eye. There were five small dimples in the stone low to his left, irregularly spaced but close enough to each other that his fingers could touch them all at once.

He almost touched the dimples, but hesitated. Something was about to happen, though he wasn't entirely sure what. He drew his hunting knife and held it firmly in his right hand, then he gingerly touched the wall.

In front of him the stone suddenly filled with golden carvings. Matthias gasped in shock, then a second later he felt like he was falling. Around him a mist filled with every color imaginable swirled.

Then it ended.

He was standing at the mouth of a cave. In front of him were the backs of six knights, their green armor patterned like leaves. Standing before them was a grey-haired man with a golden crown. Next to him was the blonde hair of his quarry.

Her gaze turned to him. For a moment their eyes held, then she took her bow from her shoulder and an arrow from her quiver.

"Wait!" Matthias exclaimed, holding up his hands to show he wasn't a threat. She drew back the bow and held it on him, and the six knights with her leveling their own weapons at him. Sweat beaded up on his brow. He let go of the dagger to further show his surrender, but his eyes never left hers.

"Stay your hands." the crowned man commanded.

Immediately the six stood to attention, though the young woman continued to aim at his heart. Matthais could see the emotions in her eyes. Anger was prominent, but also intrigue.

"Prim." the man commanded again.

She held for a moment longer before she lowered her bow with a sigh, then a slight smile turned the corner of her lips.

What is she smiling about? Matthias wondered as he lowered his hands. His focus then turned to the crowned man.

"What is your name, human?" the man asked.

"Human?" Mattias replied, then his eyes finally caught the pointed ears and sparkles of light shimmering through nearly transparent wings. "You're faeries?"

"How observant." Prim said flippantly.

"I'm surprised that I didn't notice your wings by the stream." Matthias said, not really believing what he saw. The wings hardly had any substance to them, unlike in the stories he had grown up with.

"What stream was this?" the man asked, both to Matthias and to Prim.

Matthias turned his gaze back to her. She was scared now. Matthias drew a conclusion and replied, "The one that waters the fields of Redstone, sir."

The man turned fully to Prim. She averted her gaze in shame. "What were you doing beyond our lands? You know of the old pact." His response was measured, but his voice betrayed disappointment. When she refused to reply, he asked, "You lost track of your prey, didn't you?"

Prim nodded in reply. "Yes, my king."

The king sighed in frustration, then turned to Matthias. "You still haven't given me your name, human."

Matthias stood to attention, as he would before King Thaddeus. "Matthias of Moonvale, sir."

"You should not address a king as 'sir'." he replied, a little warmth ringing in his voice.

"Then what may I call you?"

"I am King Cian, and you may refer to me as 'your grace' if you choose not to use my title. Now, how did you find the entrance to my realm? My daughter told me that she had lost your pursuit."

"She had, your grace." Matthais replied, "but I am among King Thaddeus's favorite huntsmen. I was barely able to follow her trail to the stone wall, and from there to here."

"Her trail?" asked one of the knights.

"You took a human appearance, didn't you?" King Cian rebuked angrily.

Prim bit her lip, then nodded. "I was trying to not draw suspicion, in case I ran into anyone."

"Judging by the human's presence, your plan failed." another knight said mockingly.

"Do not blame her for that." Matthias replied sternly. "I patrol the forests to catch poachers, and she is carrying a bow. I had never seen her before today and approached her as if she were poaching my king's game. Anyone else would have reacted to her differently."

The faeries were quiet for a few seconds as they thought about what he said. Matthias had watched the second knight, then turned to Prim. She was tense from the rebukes, and for good reason, but she was looking at him now with thanks in her eyes.

Matthias chose to break the silence. "What were you chasing?"

Prim dropped her gaze, then said, "I had followed a white hart beyond the bluebells. When I loosed my arrow after it, it transformed into an imp and fled." She motioned to Matthias. "It was right after that when you drew your bow on me."

"Enough." King Cian interrupted. "You will have plenty of time to discuss this later."

Matthias tensed. "What do you mean by that, your grace?"

"There are laws which must be followed. My daughter has violated a sacred law, and so have you by entering our realm."

"If I may, your grace," Matthias spoke in measured words to hide his nerves, "but I am only here because I believed her to break our own sacred laws, and I have no knowledge of your laws." He did note that Prim didn't try to counter her sentence.

"It doesn't matter." King Cian said. "Take them to the Cellar."

Matthias knew better than to fight and surrendered his bow to the knight that approached him. The knight took it, then turned back to the king. "How will he get there?"

"You will have to carry him." King Cian replied as he took to the skies. He was followed by his daughter, who was surrounded by four of the knights.

The remaining two took Matthias under each arm and rose into the air. It was not nearly as graceful as the others, but Matthias hardly noticed. It was surreal to simply fly through the air.

His eyes soon fixated on the faerie city they were headed towards, lost in the distance behind the trees of the faerie realm. It rose like a golden plant in a green vale.

Then he looked down. This was a mistake, as the sudden realization of how high up he was caused his stomach to feel weak and his head to spin. His eyes rolled back, and he fell into darkness.

When Matthias awoke from the strange dream, he realized that it hadn't been one. He sat up quietly on the silk mattress. He was in a lavish room with no windows and a single door. Evidently this was the Cellar the king had mentioned.

Makes sense, he thought. *Faeries can just fly out of a tower.*

He looked to the other corner of the room. Prim was seated on another bed with her head down, her wings wrapped along her arms and down past her thighs. The wings were more noticeable now for some reason.

Prim tilted her head up and saw that he had awoken. "Good morning." she said in a whisper.

"Is it morning already?" he asked quietly.

"You were out all night. The king will want to know that you are awake so that he can announce your sentence to the court."

"Why would he wait?"

"Faerie law requires the convicted be present before the court can decide on capital punishments," she replied, "even convictions from the king."

"What is your sentence?" Matthias was still whispering. Prim was clearly concerned that they would be heard.

"The king plans to remove my birthright as the heir."

Matthias wanted to say that he was sorry, but something was bothering him. "You keep calling Cian the king, yet he calls you his daughter."

Prim gave him a sad grin, telling him that he had guessed correctly. "He isn't my father. He married my mother when my father died, and has ruled since her death."

"If he holds such power, then why would he allow you any freedom?"

"Honestly, I doubt anyone expected him to go so far. He already made his sons the most powerful among our nobles, but to take away my birthright..." she trailed off, tears starting to form in her eyes.

Matthias crossed the room and sat beside her, placing a hand on her shoulder. "I'm sorry."

What she said next surprised him. "I need your help."

"With what?"

"You were able to enter our realm without using magic."

Matthias was confused. "I used the magic in the wall."

Now Prim was confused. "No one has been able to use that magic in generations."

"Then how did you get through?"

"I flew into the tunnel hidden behind the waterfall."

"You didn't hit the five marks?" Matthias asked while thinking. Prim suddenly flying explained the tracks, but the bardic tales were coming back to him again.

"What marks?"

Matthias suddenly had an idea. "Was the Cellar built around the same time as that tunnel?"

Prim tilted her head. "Yes. Why?"

"Did the same faerie design it?"

"No." She scoffed. "Both were made by the elf Andulan."

He knew that myth well. Andulan the Builder, who had tried to connect all the realms. But it was his son Andurou the Thief who had always captured Matthias' imagination. He could always escape from any prison.

If Andulan the elf was real, and he had built both the wall and the Cellar…

Matthias rose to his feet. First, he walked to the door, then turned and marched towards the far wall. He stopped a few feet from it and lowered himself. His eyes danced along the stonework.

Nothing to the left or right, then he looked higher.

Five dimples in the stone, of a different pattern but within a hand's width, were just visible overhead.

"Take my hand."

Prim gave him a look, then walked over and gently took his hand. He then placed his fingers on the dimples. The wall lit up in the same pattern as before, then they fell through the rainbow again. Halfway through he no longer felt her hand.

They emerged at the mouth of another cave. The sky was filled with stars, a light breeze swaying the treetops. In the distance, Matthias could see King Thaddeus's castle.

"Where are we?" Prim asked in his ear.

"That's home." Matthias said as he pointed to the castle. He turned to see her reaction to the sight, and his jaw dropped. She was barely six inches tall, standing on his shoulder with her silver wings wide open.

Prim smiled at his shock and hovered off him. "This is our normal form when in your realm."

"How was I the same size as you when I went through the wall?" he asked in wonder.

"Anyone crossing to one of the faerie realms takes on our size," she explained, "though how or why has been lost to us."

He remembered something like that from one of the bardic songs, though which one he didn't remember. "Why are your wings no longer clear?"

"Our magic is strongest in the moonlight." Prim then flew in close and kissed him on the cheek. "Thank you for helping me escape."

Matthias' cheeks burned a little. "You're welcome." Then he thought about her predicament. "What are you going to do now with your birthright gone?"

"You mean 'what will WE do'." she replied. "Cian will go to your king and demand recompense for what has happened. Neither of us is safe."

There was something in the way she said that that piqued his interest. "Well then, I know a few places we can hide, and a few more that Andurou was rumored to have visited."

"So, you'll help me regain my father's throne?"

Matthias smiled. "It is my duty to protect the forests. Your realm is within the most sacred part of the forest; therefore, I am bound by duty to it."

Prim's smile beamed in the moonlight, then a silvery mist swirled around her and grew. When it dissipated, she stood at the height he had first seen her, this time with her wings and pointed ears.

She leaned in and kissed him. "Thank you.

"MY LIFE, NO?"

Contest #31: Write a short story about someone driving home from work.

I glance to the right at the clock on my desk. It tells me it's half past five in the evening, and I've been in the office since six this morning.

I've been running all over the plant for a week, trading time between a whole line being installed, an overhead conveyor going in, and a half dozen different companies trying to fit their work around each other. Another called a day ago and moved their installation back two weeks. I have a schedule to keep, my manager wants to cut that time in half, and all my guys are stressed.

My life, no?

My gaze returns to the project chart. The delayed company's planned work still fits into my timeline should they keep to their new schedule. Another company is almost two days ahead while three others are behind in places. My team was behind earlier today, but one of my guys took advantage of another company's lunch break and got us back on track.

As to my manager's timeline, we may yet reach it. If anything is off with the electrical, and something is always off with the electrical, then we will miss the deadline.

Silently I settle for appearances. Everything will be physically done by my manager's deadline; hopefully he understands that troubleshooting is the bane of any project.

Swiftly I make out my report. Since we began this project, I have sent a daily email to all the managers as to our progress and what the next day's plans are. The first iteration takes barely a minute to type out. I've been rehearsing my words as each of today's milestones have been reached and every problem reared its head.

I read through it and make a few adjustments, then repeat the process again.

Finally, I click 'Send' and turn again to the clock. It's almost six.

With a yawn I stretch my arms and stand up. Only two more weeks of twelve-hour days before we should be done.

I take my coat from the back of my chair and turn out the lights, then at the last moment return to my computer to lock it out. I don't feel like showing up tomorrow with my computer reformatted again as an office prank, though I did come out ahead in the last war.

The parking lot is nearly empty. The second shift is here, but all the project personnel and most of management left an hour ago. I get in my old car and turn the key.

My ears are assaulted by the radio until I turn the dial down. I can't help but laugh at the daily contrast. In my office, I can listen to music at one tick above muted, but because of the car engine I need the music louder to even hear it and always forget to turn it down before I get out.

It is only a few seconds before I'm at the stop sign and turning down the road. At the second stop sign I patiently wait for a few semis, then I'm traveling down the highway. Work stays strictly in the rear-view mirror.

Now my mind is free to wander.

The sun is hanging low over the western hills, casting everything in those beautiful evening hues. I glance around at the orchards laden with fruit. I'd love to own a place like that, an orchard with a big house and room to do things.

The highway curves and I see a familiar road.

I'll be home late anyway. I think to myself as I direct the car to turn.

This way goes through the heart of the orchards. On either side I find pears, apples, and cherries in their varying ripeness. Here workers are harvesting the last of today's haul before they too go home. Over there the harvest has not started yet, but it won't be more than a few weeks.

The road dips down for a moment, then we rise to another country. The trees disappear as cattle and horses move along the pastures. One field is full of llamas.

I've never questioned it. Back home there was a corner lot with alpacas, the house across the street from them had a troop of peacocks, another on that road raised dozens of pigeons that always escaped, and the field by the racetrack had, of all things, a zebra. One field with llamas is hardly anything to pay attention to.

Above me the sky is turning purple as I hit the winding curves down the hill. At the bottom is a roaring creek along a hairpin turn. I nearly ended up in there during the winter.

The creek wasn't deep enough to swim in, but it was serene enough to meditate beside.

Another time, perhaps. Too many cougar sightings as of late to be on the creek at dusk.

I begin to puzzle at what to do with myself again. After the stress of work, I'll need a vacation. The original plan had been to visit friends down in Arizona, but a family emergency canceled that plan. Catching a flight to Boston to see the Red Sox pops into mind, but this isn't the time for it. I'd rather go at the end of the season since I've never been to Boston in the fall.

Maybe I could visit my friend in Alaska. She seemed to be enjoying herself there.

No, that would be crazy.

Guess I'll just stay home for a while.

If I could go anywhere though, where would it be? The monastery of Meteora, the Isle of Skye, or any of the more touristy parts of Europe that were always on my mind. So much history resided on the other side of the ocean, be it in Europe, Africa, or Asia. I know far more of Europe's history than the others, but Angkor Wat and Victoria Falls would also be great centerpieces for a long vacation.

Or maybe I could spend a week in NYC and catch as many Broadway productions as I could.

No, that required a year of planning. Have you tried to get decent tickets to the best Broadway shows these days? Small bit of a nightmare, especially if you're traveling with more than one other person.

The other cities in the US all have their attractions. Not being Portland is always a plus. Grew up near it, and it can keep the weird to itself as far as I'm concerned.

I almost missed the turn towards home. Fortunately, no one was coming from the other direction or waiting at the stop sign. Autopilot seems to be a little off tonight. Normally I get almost to the apartment before I need to stop daydreaming. Must be the stress from work tiring me out.

My life, no?

Whenever I think about driving on autopilot, I wonder how people would view it. I can see most people freaking out that I'm not focused on the road but am in a daydream state. It's been ten years, and I haven't hit anything yet. That's both while driving and while walking.

It's a quirk about myself that I greatly enjoy because not only do I no longer see my surroundings, but I also stop hearing the noise around me. I get to visit whatever place I want or any world I've created whenever I so choose.

All well and good, until someone tries to get my attention and can't get through the internal monologue. Another reason people would likely freak out at my autopilot skills.

I make the last turn and pull into the apartments. Within a minute, I've gotten my mail and am opening my door to be greeted by the delectable smell of a long simmering roast in the slow cooker. After checking to make sure that all the mail is indeed spam, I turn on the stove and prepare the rest of the meal.

Soon I have the potatoes peeled and sliced, corn has been taken from the freezer, and both are now boiling in their respective pots. I add salt until the taste is right and then clear the table while I wait.

Two paintings in varying stages of completion are moved to the spare room, last night's dishes are moved to the sink, and I set the music to something by Chopin. I poured a glass of milk, drink the entire thing because I was thirstier than I thought, and pour another.

The mental clock goes off. Sure enough, everything is cooked as I like it.

Once the corn and potatoes are strained, I add butter and milk to the potatoes before taking a whisk to them. A helping of potatoes goes on the plate, then I crater them and place the corn in the center. A habit I picked up in elementary school after reading a book.

The roast is then removed and cut into portions. One will be for tonight, the rest for the next few evenings.

Right before I take a bite, my phone buzzes. I recognize the tone immediately and check. I read the message, and my heart skips a beat:

Been a while since we talked. Free tonight?

My dinner is cold by the time I return to it, but a smile feels permanently fixed to my face. Alaska wasn't so crazy a plan after all.

My life, no?

"PEREGRINE"

Contest #50: Write a story told entirely through one chase scene.

The radar ping went from searching to a solid tone. I didn't need to waste a missile from the backpack launcher to take down this aircraft though. I spun right onto his tail, almost near enough to grab him.

The plasma caster would more than suffice at this range. One more enemy to take down before Highwire destroyed the final missile silo. I extended my arm and took aim.

Cloudstreak's voice came over my headset as I fired the plasma bolt. "Peregrine, enemy wingsuits at the silo!"

In an instant I dove away from the burning fighter and towards the distant silo. Above it I could see the buzzing hive of ten Etreian Archangel wingsuits. Beneath them, raining towards the ground, were the remains of Highwire and his combat squad.

I couldn't believe it, and the disbelief fed through the neural network and slowed my dive. My Aerial ReConnaissance wingsuit came to a hover as I stared at the sight, the radar contacts relegated to my subconscious.

Even before the confirmation came in from command, I watched the fiery trail streaking up from silo.

"All units: a *Blue Streak* warhead has been launched! Repeat, a warhead has been launched!"

"Command, what's the warhead's target?" I asked calmly, trying to keep my emotions in check.

"Tracking suggests its heading for Midia."

My home!

My wings responded at once, powering me towards the trail. "Command, this is Peregrine. I'm in pursuit of the warhead."

"Negative, Peregrine. We cannot confirm that this is the last warhead."

I watched as the Archangels turned to escort the warhead. My course didn't swerve. "Command, those demons are going with it. If this isn't the last warhead, they wouldn't have sent all the Archangels to escort it."

There was radio silence, so I continued moving into a pursuit angle. Mentally I kept the propulsion to super cruise. At full power an ARC suit would catch up, but this way I could at least stay within striking distance.

Etreia's *Blue Streak* missiles, in particular their second stages, are among the fastest things in the sky. Even the demons escorting it would fall behind once that stage activated. I would have to reach the missile before that happened.

The issue lay not with outrunning the first stage, but in its escort. Fighting through those Archangels with an ARC would be suicide at the best of times. They had both superior weapons and armor, and though an ARC could still take a few rounds before I had to be concerned, it would require precise aim to hit the vulnerable spots on the Archangels.

"You'll never get passed the escorts." Falcon's voice said, as if reading my thoughts again.

"Command, what other choice do we have?" Cloudstreak called out.

More seconds passed. The distance-to-target indicator stopped closing, then began to grow.

They were getting away.

Give the order, Command!

"All wingsuit units," I was already accelerating the moment I heard Command's voice, "Engage the Archangels and clear a path for Peregrine. We're uploading the warheads specs to your suits. The warhead needs to be knocked out before it gets in range of the city."

"Understood." I replied. My wings swept back, and I began to climb after the missile. Mach 2 came and went in a blur.

"Peregrine, wait for us." Cloudstreak yelled.

"Copy." I started to slow for them when the warhead data flashed onto my visor display. Quickly, I noted the model, speed, and blast radius. As I thought, it's the three-stage model.

When I saw the second stage specs though, I issued two mental commands and began accelerating again.

"Peregrine!" Falcon commanded.

I refused to respond. Falcon and the remaining suits were all true combat models. They couldn't travel at the speed of a *Blue Streak*, and this was not an ordinary *Blue Streak*. The second stage booster was vastly upgraded. Even an ARC couldn't outrun it in a straight line.

"Lieutenant, slow down!" Command ordered.

"Negative, Command." I responded. "If we don't hit it now, I'll never catch that second stage."

A pause.

"We see that now, Peregrine. No other units are close enough to intercept. Good luck."

"What the hell?" Falcon must have reached that part of the data report as well.

"Peregrine, we're counting on you." Cloudstreak said.

"Understood. I'll see you boys on the ground." I let out a slow breath. "Peregrine, going dark."

In addition to the radio, I switched off everything except life support and the passive radar to feed the propulsion. I needed every bit of power I could find, and there was no mistaking the trail left by the *Blue Streak*. The radar was only to warn me about the movement of the Archangels.

The distance indicator again stopped, then began to count down from just beyond five kilometers. Even at this range, I can make out ten Archangel wings with their distinctive golden color.

I glanced down at a new command window. It was a pair of countdowns, one for when stage two would likely deploy, the other the time until it crossed the fallout line to Midia.

My gaze jumped between it and the distance indicator to gage my window. By the time I was four kilometers out, I knew that I have a very small window before the second stage ignites. There wouldn't be much time to waste trying to dodge any of the escorts, much less fight them.

I shifted the wing configuration to minimize my drag. My closing speed increased, but it didn't add much to the window. We'd already sailed past Mach 3. Covering almost two miles every three seconds, even a hundred miles per hour was becoming a miniscule difference.

I then looked to the indicator for my plasma caster. Before the shutdown of its feed to the power supply, the caster had stored three charges. I also had the pair of very short-range air-to-air missiles left in the backpack launcher, but they were of little use. We were now moving faster than they flew.

Still, both weapon commands had gone off without a hitch.

The passive radar blared. A quick glance told me why. About half of the demons had slowed to engage me. The remaining five were still managing to keep up with the *Blue Streak*, though they would soon be left behind by that second stage booster.

For a moment I panicked, then I recognized that their closing speed was too great. They'd only have one pass at me before I zoomed past them.

Two of the demons seemed to notice this mistake and tried to accelerate back towards the warhead, but it was too late. The others fired their plasma casters, machine guns, and even a few missiles at me.

Some callsigns are demanded.

Some are given in jest.

Some, like mine, are earned. No one can maneuver an ARC at full speed like I can.

Even so, I felt the impact of bullets bouncing off my armor, the only saving grace at this speed being the glancing angle they impacted me at. One plasma charge narrowly missed my head, a guaranteed fatal strike, and even so I was blind for a few seconds until my eyes recovered.

Mentally I set the autopilot to hold heading, and when I could see again, I was only a few degrees off course, and half of my foes were now behind me.

When I glanced forward, I suddenly noticed that two of the remaining Archangels began to rapidly decelerate and fall, taking a few shots at me before they jettisoned their wings. Clearly, they had run out of power.

I looked at my own power supply indicator. Only 34% remained, and I had started the chase with a little over 60%.

Though I could ill afford it, I set the autopilot again and ran a quick diagnostic. One line in my left wing was shorting out from bullet damage. I cut off the node and the freefall of power slowed at 28% left. I was still consuming vast amounts of energy trying to catch up, but now I could catch the warhead before I ran out.

I may have to bail out for once.

One of the three demons slowed to engage me. This guy knew what he was doing, only decelerating enough that he could come alongside me and pick me apart at his leisure.

That he wasn't using his gun told me that either he'd run out of ammo attacking Highwire and was closing to plasma range, or he didn't want to miss. I bet on the latter.

I deftly moved the plasma caster into a forward position by sliding my arm up my torso and pressing my wrist to my shoulder. The Archangel didn't seem to notice.

The range on a plasma caster is a little more than 500 meters before the charge loses integrity and dissipates. We reached that range and continued to close.

Waiting for the easy shot, then.

I turned on the targeting assist, taking aim at the demon's head. More power diverted, but necessary if I was to succeed.

At 300 meters I made a shift to the left and readied to fire. The Archangel fired first, narrowly missing my shoulder as he put a hole in my wing. My charge hit the Archangel's visor, and he disappeared behind me.

I check the distance. Just over two kilometers to go.

The last two Archangels were flying as fast as they could while they fire sporadically at me with machine gun rounds. I felt a few bullet impacts, but the range was far enough for my subtle dodging to throw off their aim.

Now within two kilometers. I only had two shots remaining in the plasma caster, and two Archangels remained in my way.

The demons began to slow. I couldn't afford to waste my plasma bolts on them, but I had to survive this encounter in order to even get close enough for the opening to take out the *Blue Streak*.

Either way, they're now in plasma caster range.

Autopilot became a must as I closed my eyes and issued a mental command. Autopilot began evading the incoming fire while the active radar switched on and pinged the Archangels in front of me.

The two split apart, then realized their mistake.

It was too late.

A few more rounds struck my wings, but the Archangels were now out of position. I'd zoom right between them.

Even so, I couldn't pass up the chance for another kill with my more expendable ordinance.

The data was transferred to the pack, which opened and armed the two missiles. Once I heard the tone indicating the missiles are ready, I spun and fired.

I barely felt the small charge that pushed the missiles away from me before they ignited their engines. Then I zoomed past the last Archangels.

The radar confirmed that I hit one, the missiles flying through a second after I'd cleared the airspace.

At first, I accepted that I missed the other, but then I noticed the error message. My last missile was jammed and stuck to my back in the open position.

Closing the pack with an active weapon was a fool's choice, but I couldn't afford the drag. The pack closed with its potential timebomb, and I continued to close in.

I was now less than a kilometer out, but my wings were in bad shape. My display indicated I was only capable of 82% output with the varied plasma and bullet impacts. Even so, I was still gaining on the warhead.

Nothing but time stood against me. With the diminished speed, my window was now seconds at best.

I readied the plasma caster. The range was fast approaching.

Ten seconds. 750 meters.

I moved the plasma caster into position, pressing my wrist to my shoulder.

Six seconds. 660 meters.

The *Blue Streak*'s first stage shuts down and decouples in one moment.

Two seconds. 570 meters.

The second stage ignited. I fired both charges at its engines from extreme range. The first slipped just behind the flames, but the second smashed between two engines. The entire section exploded.

My wings spread out to help me maneuver around the debris. I mentally turned the radio back on. "Command, this is Peregrine."

The joy was brief. I saw the blue flames of the final third stage ignite. The destruction of the second stage must have caused the warhead to trigger a failsafe.

I cleared the debris and resumed my chase. "Second stage was destroyed. The final stage activated and is still on course. Attempting to pursue."

I started to hear celebration in that background at Command from my first sentence, but by the end of my report the background was silent. "Acknowledged, Peregrine."

"Going dark." I turned on the active radar for a brief moment. The gap was widening, and I was already at my full output.

I looked again at the timer. It had been right about the second stage; now there was only the countdown to my home's demise. I issued a command about the third stage. The data showed that it wasn't as fast as the second, but it was still too fast with my ARC not at full flight capacity.

Come on! There must be a way. My eyes danced between the command windows. The distance was already back to one kilometer, and even with my wings configured to minimize drag again, I was barely gaining on the warhead.

I took a quick glance at the timer. Three minutes to the boundary.

I ran through the calculations in my head, then I had the computer check as I ran through them again.

Both say the same thing.

300 meters short.

I won't make it.

I could turn off life support and throw everything into speed, but I would pass out long before I reached firing range. Even if I could get there in time, I had nothing but a service pistol and a jammed missile to take the thing down with.

The jammed missile!

I sent the command for the pack to open the loading flap. This helps the techs load the missiles, but now it's turned the pack into a booster.

So long as the missile doesn't launch inside the pack and blow me up.

The command was given. I feel the surge and have the suit adjust for the new propulsion system. The calculation numbers on the visor slowly ticked down.

200 meters short.

100 meters.

Just enough.

The missile ran out of fuel, and I was back to just my own power. I checked the display one final time. There was now a five second window to knock out the warhead. After that, radiation would hit the city.

I looked at the timer.

Thirty seconds.

Using my service pistol was out of the question. I was flying faster than the bullet would travel. I'd only be shooting at myself.

The missile was also useless now.

Fifteen seconds.

Only one option. I hated it, and I probably wouldn't survive it.

My wingsuit creeped over the engines as I spread my wings to full extent. The drag started to slow me, but I needed as much striking area as possible.

I dove at the engines and gave the ARC one final command.

Release wings.

I almost blacked out from the deceleration, and the shockwave from the explosion left me fuzzy. Shrapnel wounds stung where my armor got punctured, but as I spun through the air, I caught sight of the *Blue Streak*.

The kamikaze worked. The warhead was thrown clear of the explosion, but it was falling well short of its mark into the desert south of Midia.

I rotated in the air to control my descent like a skydiver, directing my fall to carry me away from the explosion. A few minutes later, as I pulled the chute, the warhead detonated harmlessly in the Midian Desert.

The light was blinding, but by then I was out of range.

A rescue helicopter followed my emergency transmitter and picked me up a few hours later. Needless to say, I was commended for my actions and even given a promotion.

The war ended before my shrapnel wounds healed, but I did manage to get back to flying again.

It'll take more than a collision with a nuke to clip this peregrine's wings.

"BLACKOUT"

Contest #58: Write about someone who purposefully causes a power outage.

Tanager quietly slid out of the vent, then looked for the access panel Thrasher had briefed her on.

Her role in the operation was simple compared to the others. After the halo drop, she'd made her way into the main power station, where she would wait for Thrasher's program to let her disable the power to the entire complex.

Once both Thrasher and Whydah had secured the data they were here for, she would plunge the base into darkness and the team would escape without casualties.

The panel opened easy enough, but before starting her role she used her night vision glasses to find the main maintenance door. One twisted pipe later, that door was braced from any sudden intrusion.

Tanager set down her pack and pulled out one of the pistols and her tablet. The tablet lit up as soon as the wires were connected. Thrasher' program was already consuming the system. She started keying in the shutdown sequence. Everything was going according to plan.

She saw a few random codes go out. Most she recognized as encrypted orders, something the hackers would have a field day with. Others were simple commands.

One in particular caught her attention: Stardust.

Interesting name.

"Cardinal to Tanager, status."

Tanager put a hand to her earpiece. "In the vault, awaiting confirmation on data retrieval."

"Understood, Tanager." That was Bunting, the XO for the operation and Tanager's former mentor. That he had replied to the open comm was another reassurance that everything was according to plan. He would soon switch to receiving only, listening for any last-second hiccups.

"How's Whydah doing?" she asked quickly before Bunting signed off.

"Using his sharp eye." Bunting replied. "He found a second data server that he's trying to access."

"Understood." Tanager smiled. Though he was the newest member of the team,

Whydah fit in quickly. While he wasn't up to Thrasher's skill in hacking, the young man was the best candidate for tackling a target of opportunity.

At least, if he were caught, he'd have little to say. He hadn't even seen Eden Base yet.

Or Syreen. Tanager had promised she would show him her home when the war ended.

Not now. "Cardinal, make sure he knows that we are t-minus four minutes to blackout."

"Copy." Only Cardinal had full comms access during an operation. That way if anyone was caught, it would only trace to him. No one ever knew where Cardinal was during an operation.

Fitting for a former member of the Spectre Corp.

Tanager turned to her tablet and looked over the sequences. Thrasher's program had reached 92% of the grid. Once she triggered the shutdown, power would be lost to nearly the entire facility.

Only a few facilities were untouched by the code. Concerningly, these included the north auto turret command center.

Right along our primary escape route.

Her eyes dropped to the extraction diagram. A helo was marked for extraction and Bunting would already be joining the heavy units inside. They would escape to the south once the lights turned off.

She, Thrasher, and Whydah would make their way north or west with hard copies of the intel. Satellite downloading had been difficult to send securely as of late.

The number refused to rise, and she checked the watch again. T-minus three minutes. When she looked back, the percentage had decreased. The western auto turrets were now coming back online!

"Cardinal, western turrets are back online." She tried to report calmly. "Someone's combating Thrasher's program."

"Understood, Tanager. Stand by."

Her heart beat loudly several times. No one had caught Thrasher yet. His skills were infallible.

Still, she saw that there was a way to reach the western extraction point. If she were to follow -

A message took over her screen. "GOODBYE, TANAGER."

Tanager stared at the message for a moment. It felt like an eternity. Not only had they been discovered, but whoever it was knew her signal. That could only mean one thing: a traitor!

She frantically started the shutdown sequence. "Cardinal, Code Black! We've been had!"

It was only a moment before she heard Cardinal on the open frequency. "All units: exfil now!"

Tanager heard boots thumping on metal. *They're already outside!* "Preparing to drop the grid." She called over the open comms. "Good luck."

A voice called out behind the maintenance door as she keyed in the final code. The door moved a crack before the brace caught it. The metal rattled each time guards tried to force it open. A worthless glance told her that the brace was failing, a moment lost to finish the sequence.

The brace failed. The door swung open.

She disconnected, grabbed her pack, and leapt towards the roof access ladder.

The already dark accessway went completely black for a moment, but then it came alive in a flashing storm of bullets.

Many missed her by slim margins, but she survived unscathed. She pulled down her night vision glasses from the cover of a beam and took a worried glance. At least a dozen shapes were moving towards her. The guards didn't have vision glasses, but they didn't turn on their flashlights either. Instead, they stared down their sights and scanned the room.

Thermal or night vision sights. Tanager sorely hoped for the latter and pulled out her pistol. She was the only thermal signature in the enclosure. *Still...*

She reached into her pack, feeling for the right cylinder. Once she found it, she quickly pulled the pin and tossed it into the midst of the guards. Then she closed her eyes and covered her ears.

The moment the flashbang went off, she sprang into action. She fired three times, downing a man with each shot. Then she threw the pistol past the guards as her hand caught the ladder. The pistol clattered out the door, and even in their haze the guard heard the noise and fired towards it.

She continued to climb silently as the guards chased her phantom. By the time they had discovered her ruse and were shooting at the ladder, she was closing the hatch.

Taking her spare pistol from the pack, she made a quick scan of the scene. Vehicles and men were hurrying around, and several helos were already airborne. She wondered if Bunting's had taken off.

"Bunting, what's your status?"

Nothing. Not even static.

"Cardinal, status?"

Still nothing.

She looked down at her receiver. At least one bullet had punctured it. From its angle, the bullet would have blasted her hip had the receiver not been there.

She was alive, but she was deaf.

Tanager got off the roof as quickly as possible, then she hurried to the back of a moving jeep and jumped onto its bumper. Several others were also hanging off the back with her.

"Where are the other intruders?" she asked them.

"Sounds like most of the remaining ones are in the lab." the nearest guard said. "Some made for the airfield, but we got their leader pinned by the north wall."

Cardinal's been sighted? If it were true, then the traitor had to be someone on the team itself!

"You guys got the Birds in the station?" the guard asked her.

She shook her head. "They slipped onto the roof. I couldn't get a shot off."

"Fine by me." another replied. "That Tanager is supposed to be quite the looker. I'd like to be one of the ones interrogating her before the Bureau shows up."

"I'm sure you would." Tanager replied. Not the first time she'd heard that sentiment, but never in the middle of an active area of operation.

An explosion roared overhead. "LOOK OUT!"

Tanager looked up to see a ball of fiery metal falling towards them. She leapt from the back and rolled. The guards hanging on beside her jumped as well, but those in the jeep were crushed before they could escape the crashing helo.

The impact rang in her ears, but she got to her feet quickly and gazed at the inferno. One body had been thrown clear. Though their face was charred beyond recognition, she saw the patch of Eden on the agent's shoulder.

"Where'd that come from?" one of the guards asked. Tanager turned to see three rising from their tumble, and she could hear footsteps behind her.

"That guy's a Mornovian! See his patch."

Tanager then caught the look in one of the guards' eyes, the look of one connecting the dots. She heard someone else yell, "Tanager!", before she fired. All three guards fell without getting a shot at her.

She turned to fire at the guards behind her, shots coming from her left as she did. There was only one guard left, slumping to his knees. The others were dead on the ground.

Tanager looked in the direction of the shots. She recognized Whydah at once, his black coat stylized with shin-length tails reminiscent of his codename. "What are you doing here?" she asked.

"They got the others in the lab." Whydah replied sternly as he hurriedly holstered his pistol and grabbed two of the assault rifles, tossing the first one to her. "Thrasher isn't responding to my calls. I was worried when you weren't either and went to find you."

"A bullet hit my receiver." Tanager said. Whydah wasn't normally so serious, even in such a circumstance. "Any word from Cardinal?"

"He made it out, though he's drawing them to the south. An ARCAPES wing is nearby and will provide cover if we get to our extraction point in the north."

She felt a glimmer of hope. "Which recon squad is in the ARCAPES?"

Whydah finished inspecting the rifle and put a hand to his ear. "Cardinal, this is Whydah. I've located Tanager and we are exfiltrating. Which squads are we looking for?" He waited for the reply. "Understood." He turned to her with a slight grin. "You knew the Five-Tenth was nearby, didn't you?"

"I'd heard they were in the area." She replied.

"From Peregrine, right?" Whydah's grin widened as he mentioned the ARC flier. "We might just get out of this alive."

He handed her a flash drive. "I made two hard copies of the data. Best that we each take one."

"Anything useful?"

"*Blue Streaks* with nuclear warheads are ready to launch from Sarahela." Whydah replied, his voice deathly serious. "I wasn't able to verify the targets."

Oh my God! "Then let's hurry." Tanager replied with false calm as she took the lead. She went west, using the dry drainage bed that she had seen before the message had appeared. The two hurried as quickly and unassumingly as they could.

She thought about Whydah's discovery. There was little wonder why his jovial nature had vanished. If ever there was a missile to be feared, the *Blue Streak* was Etreia's candidate. Few things were faster in the sky, and only a railgun or a top rate ARC flier could pose a real threat to shooting one down.

To add a nuke, though? Etreia must be getting desperate.

She could think of a half dozen coalition cities that they could strike with ease from Sarahela; beautiful Katlov in Mornovia, her home city of Syreen in far Atlanae, the feisty city-state of Midia. Even Eden Base. All of them could be destroyed if the defense networks failed to stop the missiles.

They reached the west wall without further incident. An electric grate had dropped to guard the drainage exit, but with the power dead they made quick work of it.

They'd made it out.

They had almost lost sight of the west wall when a bullet struck Whydah and he fell. Tanager turned and fired a burst at the perpetrator. He fell from view with at least two shots to the chest. She hit all four of his friends when they tried to return fire.

Tanager turned to Whydah. He wasn't moving and a pool of blood was forming under his head.

"Amare!" She cried his name as she knelt beside him. He couldn't die yet. Not when they were so close.

She gently lifted his head and felt the wound. It was gushing blood as any head wound would, but the bullet hadn't breached Whydah's skull.

Tanager sighed in relief, then used Whydah's receiver as she tore off a sleeve to wrap the wound. "Cardinal, Whydah's hit. I need extraction on my location ASAP."

"They're on their way." Came the reply a moment later. "Command needs that data. Hold tight."

"Understood." She lifted Whydah and carried him behind a fallen tree that might provide some cover. For a few tense minutes she watched for any more Etreians, hoping that Peregrine and the Five-Tenth would reach them soon.

Then she heard a noise from behind. She turned her gun towards the sound, but lowered it when she saw the familiar face.

"Thrasher, -" Tanager exclaimed, until she saw the hacker lift the gun towards them. It all clicked. "You?"

"I must say that I'm impressed that you still got the power off in time." Thrasher said as he slowly walked to her. "The Kingdom could have used you."

"Why?" she pleaded. "Why would you betray us when Etreia is about to-"

"Because I *am* Etreian. That orphan story was a pleasant fantasy to play to your emotions."

Tanager was stunned. "But you have killed thousands of your own people!"

"And over twenty times that of yours." He replied with a wicked grin. "Now it all will end with the destruction of your 'great' coalition and her cities."

"What about the defense networks?"

"What about 'em? You saw the signal of my masterpiece, yes? Stardust? It shut down the defense grids. Everything lost power. Even if your home countries tried to surrender, they wouldn't be able to send the signal."

"You're a madman!" Tanager yelled. "All those people will die!"

"It will save far more in the end." Thrasher said matter-of-factly. "I can assure you of that. No one will have the stomach to fight us after that slaughter. As for you, there are no units near enough to save you, and no one near enough to stop the launch, so I'll give you one chance to save Whydah's life. Surrender."

"Never." Whydah's faint voice croaked. Tanager looked down at him as he slowly tried to rise. For a moment, she could only feel joy that he was still alive.

"A pity." Thrasher said, and as Tanager turned back to him, she saw the barrel level on Whydah.

"NO!"

It was a booming voice, one projected from a wingsuit's crowd control speaker. As they all turned up to it, a flash of wings zoomed through the trees and struck the ground. Thrasher cried out as he was crushed by the ARC suit, and before he could say anything coherent a plasma bolt fired.

The ARC turned around as more wingsuits landed, others flying south to hopefully find Cardinal. "You alright, Beth?" Peregrine asked.

She nodded. "Just in time, Felix."

"Keep to formalities, you two." Highwire commanded as he and several other Jaegers walked up to them.

"Those are some nasty wounds." Cloudstreak said as she knelt beside them. She then extended her plasma caster and held it to Tanager's arm. Tanager gritted her teeth as the searing heat sealed the wound. "That should work until we return to base."

"There's no time!" Whydah said as another Jaeger treated his head wound more gently. "Etreia is preparing to launch nuclear-tipped *Blue Streaks*."

"Where?" Peregrine replied quickly, his wingsuit already humming.

"Cardinal said you have the launch data." Highwire said to Whydah.

They both handed him their drives. "These have all that we were able to collect."

"It'll have to be enough." Highwire inserted the drives into his suit and began uploading the data to Command.

Tanager turned to Peregrine. "I'm glad you were in the area."

She heard his brief laugh. He was trying to stay calm while they waited for orders. "I'm glad you caught on to the turncoat's scheme when you did."

"I wish I'd caught him sooner."

"I know." Peregrine replied somberly. "At least you're safe."

"Any word on the *Blue Streaks*?" Whydah interjected.

"Command has a preliminary on it." Highwire stated. His suit started to hum. "They want us to scramble now."

"No support, I take it?" Peregrine asked as though he was certain there would be none.

"Correct. The Five-Tenth and the Hundred-n-Third will destroy the missile silos while the Four-Fifteenth extracts the agents."

"Then let's scramble." Peregrine said as he launched into the air. Falcon was right behind him, as were the others from their squads.

Highwire turned to Whydah's medic. "You have command, Redfin."

"Understood. We'll get them home." he said, then he took Whydah in his arms and flew off with his Jaegers.

"Tanager."

She turned to see Highwire and Cloudstreak lifting their visors. "Anything you want us to tell Felix?"

Tanager paused as another Jaeger came to carry her off. "Tell him to stop the *Blue Streaks*."

The two shared a look. "Anything else?" Cloudstreak asked.

"If you fail, there may not be anything else. I'll talk with him once you've succeeded."

Cloudstreak started to press her further, but Highwire cut her off. "I'm sure he'll understand that. You did well to get the intel for us. We'll see that it isn't wasted." The two then took off to join their squads.

Tanager turned to the remaining Jaeger. "Ready when you are, Flashback."

Flashback laughed. "Don't take this the wrong way, but I hope this is the last time I have to carry you out like this."

She smiled, put her arms around his neck, and then they took off.

The support helo for the Four-Fifteenth had ventured close enough for a quick drop-off, but the entire flight she noticed neither the chill of the air nor the chatter between the Jaeger team. Her mind was on the ARC going after the missiles.

Godspeed, Peregrine.

"THE REMEMBERED PAST"

Contest #61: Write about a character who smells something familiar and is instantly taken back to the first moment they smelled it.

My God, how it's changed.

It wasn't the first time the thought had crossed my mind on this business trip. The old capital had a rich history that was for the most part spared during the Great Fire thanks to the ancient canals and sheer cliffs surrounding the Palace District, where the royal palace, St. Ambrose's Cathedral, and the Order of the Kestrel's citadel stood prominent over the countryside.

However, the Great Fire had burned much of the Heights District and the densely populated Satin Row, and the food riots in the aftermath had ravaged everything from downtown to the harbor.

That was five years ago, and you'd need to go five years farther back to my only other visit to Talisae.

I caught sight of a street I knew and begrudgingly turned down it. The marks from the fire were gone, but the old medieval buildings in the Heights were swiftly being replaced by the architecture of modernity. Hard concrete replaced handmade brick and carved wood. Malls with modern ideas were taking over the traditional shops. Promises to remember and preserve the past were forgotten for the sake of progress.

Ten years ago. A magical time in my life, yet aside from the Palace District, it seemed like everything I remembered from that trip had faded into history.

Another street remembered. Another turn.

Clothing had long since changed from the ancient days of the buildings, but the decade of trials had changed the attitude of the people. Groups walked with their faces looking at screens and blocking out the world around them. Ten years ago, a cell phone would have been a rarity as everyone greeted those they passed by.

A problem not unique to Talisae, but it broke the old magic even further.

Another turn.

I catch a scent on the air. It brings me to a halt. I take in several deep breaths to confirm it isn't a false memory, then I follow it.

My spirit lifts as I see the centuries-old building hiding between two modern neighbors, somehow spared the ravages of time. All the outdoor seating is full, and when I walk inside, they only have a single space left at the bar. I took it eagerly, and set myself down once again in the stronghold of the White Rose Tavern & Inn.

I'd read that it had been damaged in the fire, that some developer wanted to tear it down, that it had been on the verge of closing forever. The signs of such things were not present in the bustling establishment. I asked the bartender about those things as I ordered. She replied that the White Rose had survived thanks to some old academics that had purchased the building and were in the process of getting it registered as a historical site.

I drank heartily to that with a few nearby locals and tourists.

It was a few minutes later when the wave of nostalgia crested. A local came in yelling that the national team had won the Cup and the entire place broke into singing the anthem. I joined in the words until my small order was placed in front of me. I took one whiff, and the world faded.

We had visited Talisae on a school trip. It was the week before Labor Day, and our club was starting our senior year off with a bang. It had taken about two years of planning and saving to afford the overseas flights and lodgings, and a couple months of convincing a few of our parents that we would honestly be on the return flights.

I was explicitly told to keep an eye on Sandra and Brodie by her father, who was also my pastor at the time. No one, at least that I know of, was told to keep an eye on me.

The first day had been strictly left to finding our bearings in the great city, and a guide had told us about the White Rose and the dancing that would be held the next night, with local musicians playing the old songs. At the behest of the girls in the group, I taught the rest of the guys the basics of a few once we called it a day and were back at the hotel.

From the next morning until the evening, we explored all over the Palace District, walking through the thousand-year-old cathedral and marveling at the splendor of ancient kings. Then, as the sun was low in the sky, we went to the White Rose, and that's where I met Rhea.

It had the appearance of a chance meeting as we both took a break from dancing with our own friends. In truth, my thoughts had been captive to her since I'd first seen her, and her thoughts were likewise on me, which we both confessed as the conversation started.

After asking where each other was from, the bartender asked if we wanted anything. I was content with just water, but she insisted I have a local pastry with her. I couldn't very well refuse. It smelled almost as good as it tasted. Once we had finished, a waltz started, and we danced together.

I've never had anyone follow my lead as well as Rhea did that night. Even if she broke the rule that she must be looking over my shoulder to be in proper form, we glided across the floor with only those bright eyes and wide smile in my sight. The only thing that existed in that moment was us and the music.

It wasn't until the music faded that we realized that everyone else had left the floor and the musicians had kept up the tune three times longer than the composer had written.

We were both a little embarrassed by the attention, but having everyone clamor to dance with us afterwards made up for it. And yet, by the end of the night, we had danced together another dozen times.

Midnight had long passed when we parted ways, promising to meet again in the morning. With Sandra and Brodie accounted for, I got everyone to the hotel, and we quickly fell asleep.

The others rolled out of bed sometime in the late morning. To their surprise, and to a few late risers' horror, I had been up since dawn. I'd never needed much sleep when adventure was near. I always tried to be the last one asleep and the first awake.

Rhea, too, had this quality. We'd already met for breakfast in the White Rose, sharing again the local pastry.

The anthem fades, and I return from the memories to the pastry in front of me. I catch my fingers playing with the ring on my hand. Rhea's wearing its twin back home, likely waking the kids so that they can make it to school on time. I can't help but smile as I take a picture and send it to her.

Even with all that's changed in the last decade, I will always remember the day I met you.

Love you.

"OF LADIES AND TIGERS"

Contest #62: Write about two characters on the verge of a life-changing event, but one has rigged the outcome. (Inspired by and heavily referencing Frank R. Stockton's The Lady, or the Tiger? from 1882. Highly recommend reading his story.)

I sat in my moonlit cell filled with dread for the coming dawn. Soon after the morning rays broke the horizon, I would be taken to the arena and presented with two choices; behind one of the ever-changing doors would be a ravenous tiger, the other concealed a fair maiden of the king's choosing.

I have seen justice from the arena many times. One could not deny the fairness of the ordeal, for it was only by the criminal's own hand that he faced death or life.

There were many doors leading into the circular arena, and when the time came, a torch would light over two of them. The accused would then make his fateful choice. Open the tiger's door and his death was certain; open the maiden's door and he would be wed to her on the spot.

It was also not so simple as to walk up to one door and inspect it, then turn to the other if the first seemed deadly. The king had made certain that the arena's doors could not be used to tell what lay beyond.

One man, a respected scholar who had made the mistake of challenging the king's legitimacy, had spent nigh on an hour before each door before he made his choice. A tiger had greeted him.

Another, the town drunk who had made the inebriated mistake of pissing on the king's carriage, had walked right up to his door and opened it. He too met the tiger, but his drinking partner did the exact same the next day and now has four children.

There was no great feat of intelligence needed to survive the arena. It was simply a matter of instinct for the accused.

A most barbarian method, but one with some form of polish.

One I had never wanted to be part of.

What crime had led me here? No worthy crime have I ever committed, except the crime of loving a woman.

Though born a common peasant, I had caught the eye of the princess some months ago, and we had become fast friends. She proved both cunning and jealous, finding ways to slip out of her court to seek me in secret, and knowing the fullness of what I did when we were apart.

We made love and spoke often of running away. She confided in me matters of state, and I saw several of my suggestions make their way into her father's laws. She and her trusted handmaidens knew of my family and a few close friends, though their true identities were concealed.

What a thrill it was to have the princess by my side!

I dare say that it would have gone further still, even to some faraway land, if we had not been caught by some missed step or another. On our last rendezvous, we were cornered like rats and taken by the king's guards to face sentencing.

The king, from whom the princess had inherited her cunning, would not punish her directly. He loved her too much to send her to the arena, but that was where I presented an opportunity. She was told to sit at his side as he passed the sentence onto her lover. I was swiftly sent to the cells and the arena was made ready.

I see that the sky is beginning to turn, and I think to the princess. She would surely find some way by which to determine what lay behind each door. She would stop at nothing less than knowing that answer. Then, from her seat beside the king, when all eyes were on me, she would signal to the door I should take. I was certain of this mercy.

And yet, her jealousy remained, and so the choice of trust was voided to me.

Had I not discovered her jealousy, I would have faced the day without such anxiety. Now, knowing it, I could not help but dwell upon it.

Could she abide me being wed to another, one who must surely be of lower station than herself? I had even heard a rumor passing through the cells that the maiden chosen was from among the handmaidens who knew of our secret.

The knowledge brought less comfort, for the princess would then lose me to a trusted friend no less, perhaps even the one who had given away our rendezvous.

Rumors all, and yet all I had to cling to were rumors and speculation. If today were not the day, I might well worry myself to death trying to understand the mind of the princess.

Cunning would unveil the doors, but would love or jealousy win?

The guards came to the door almost the moment the sun's rays entered my cell. One last touch of peace before I faced my fate.

They led me through the darkened tunnel that connected the cells to the arena. I saw the bright opening long before we reached it, and when I stepped through, it was to the cheer of thousands.

It was no surprise that so many would come to see my judgment. My crime involved no less than the princess, after all. No greater intrigue had ever graced the arena before, and they all wanted to see what judgment declared.

The king gave a command, and two torches were lit on the far side. The doors were right beside each other this time. The special doors that emitted no sound or odor, the doors that gave no hint as to what lay behind.

Despite myself, I waved to the crowd. It was a superstition that those who played to the crowd might win the favor of fate, that those who showed a disdain for death would not face the tiger. A superstition that had failed many times, though admittedly those seemed few and far between whenever the memories were brought to mind.

The crowd cheered, and admittedly I gained confidence from their voices.

After appeasing fate, I turned to the king, seated in his royal box that moved between each visit to the arena. As I knew she would be, the princess was seated beside him with her handmaidens.

One was missing.

The princess was paler than normal. Was it because she worried about my fate? Did it mean she was submitting me to the tiger? Or was she pale because she would surrender me to another, and jealousy was fighting for control?

I gave a bow, then lifted my eyes to her. Her hand made a gesture to the right, so subtle that it would seem like nothing to anyone else. There was no hesitation in her command.

My mind was made in that instant, foolishly or not. I turned and walked confidently to the door on the right. I reached the door and threw it open with a simple question in mind:

Did love or jealousy win?

"AUTUMNAL FIRE"

Contest #63: Start your story with the line, "By the time I stepped outside, the leaves were on fire." (Whether this is a literal fire is up to you.)

By the time I stepped outside, the leaves were on fire. The winter lockdown had extended so long that it stole the blooming spring, and then it stole the joys of summer, but now with the maples turning to their blazing orange, I was finally free.

As a society we came close to losing our minds from forced isolation. Some pessimists still claim it is a flash in the pan, that the iron bars will swing shut again. It is not an idle thought. The killer still lurks out there, and our leaders continue to fear it, right or wrong.

For me though, I wanted to make the most of the opportunity before the bars might swing again. If they did, then I'd have a taste to cling to as the winter months closed in. If not, then I'd have a head start on those waiting for certainty.

Either way, the desire of the new and of connection is nigh inexorable.

Not that my time in isolation hasn't been productive. To the contrary, a bachelor in his home can only be idle for so long before things need to get done, before his thoughts turn to creating and growing. With nothing open for society to do after I got off from work, I let more of the old Renaissance or perhaps Victorian mentality slip through, that of the lone man in his study, left to the devices of his mind and how to bring that which he conjures into the physical world.

Some nights I would sit by the canvas and paint the landscapes that formed in my mind. The sun rising over fog covered hills, a sailing ship cruising in front of the rising moon, a snowcapped mountain towering over the trees. The first pieces I attempted were frustrating to be sure, as the paint refused to cooperate with my imagination. As more time was spent with the brush, the paint grew more familiar and flowed as I desired, beginning to draw out the worlds that my mind loved to explore.

Truthfully I would never claim equality with any of the old masters; that would require many years to even approach those I idolize.

Twice I tried to paint figures, bringing people I pictured into being, but those pieces are best kept private as I learn proper proportions. Again, the diligence of practice will eventually lead me to where such art could become worthy of public eyes. At least, in my estimation of what is worthy for public consumption.

The same story dwelled in my foray into music; early frustrations that gave way to some form of competence. Admittedly this was a late and oft neglected addition to my routine, and so little can be claimed from it.

Other nights were spent lying back in my chair with a book, a cup of tea or a mug of cocoa resting on the end table. My personal library had exploded in the intervening months of seclusion, fueled by the simplicity of 'adding to cart'.

I learned the art of power, wrestled with the doctrines of Spurgeon, marveled at the life of Rockefeller, sailed the Barbary Coast with the Sea Hawk, flew to far away galaxies, and journeyed alongside the myths of olden days. I revisited old tales that I had almost forgotten, and found new favorites that I must tell others about; the tales from Tolkien's realm of Faerie, the exploration in Steele's *Coyote*, the classic tale of *Dune*, and the great plays of Shakespeare.

Long as well did I explore the wisdom of the past. To satisfy my love of the intricacies of war I learned of those whose actions led to the Great War, delved further still into the complexities of the Thirty Years War, and jumped furthest back to the time of the Diodachi's wars. Plato explained how his ideal republic would be run, Cicero tried in vain to save his republic, and the Stoics instructed on how to model life. My education was finished with explorations into Jung psychology and the works of C. S. Lewis.

I also added my own stories to the collection as the summer days waned, taking part in writing contests and even publishing for the first time. It was a small book, barely more than fifty pages, but an accomplishment to build upon, nonetheless. Worlds of my own creation were entering the public sphere; worlds that others may also take interest in.

But now my isolation has ended. As the world opened, I planned to venture far and wide. The mountains of Montana, the coasts of Oregon, and the deserts of Arizona were all given their dates and purchases. Far flung expeditions to Europe were discussed with friends that would hold such interest, visiting the sites of old battlefields and the homes of famous foods and landmarks. Japan built a to-scale model of a beloved mecha, and I mapped out the journey required to reach it.

This is the world I've been waiting to return to. Books, music, painting; all of it reminds us of and inspires us about the wonders of our planet. Though I can see pictures and videos of the great locales, those cannot convey the place in its entirety.

The smell of the mighty sea or the mystical forest, the feeling of the wind in your hair or the cold snow on your cheeks, the taste of the cuisine passed down from ancient times. Even the farthest flung galaxies or the wildest fantasy realms are built on truths learned from that which lay outside our doors.

This may only be a moment, but it is one that must be taken. Though I sojourn alone in many places as I tease out new experiences for those I'll bring along later, the journey is best when shared.

Sometimes it is a group of friends separated since college who reunite through common interest in an event.

Other times it's reconnecting with the family we've missed that have moved to the far corners of the land.

Still others, and some may argue to them being the best, are shared with the strangers who become fast friends as we explore wonders unexpected.

Sometimes even love is found on such endeavors.

And so, I sojourn while I can and pray for the day when we can sojourn unimpeded. Let this autumnal fire ignite the passion that will bring us all together once the day finally comes and the long winter has subsided.

"JEALOUS FLAMES"

Contest #63: Write a romance that involves one partner saving the other from a fire. (Probably not very romantic...)

Helena was roused by the sentry's horn. Before she could rise Astor had somehow cleared his own bed and was already tying his quiver to his armor. The past several nights they had worn their armor to sleep as the threat of attack loomed over Serenisa. "Which horn?" she asked him.

"Sounded like Gerould's." Astor replied. A moment later the sound came again, and Helena saw him frown. "Yep. I can hear that hole in his horn from here."

"The ice spider caves?" Helena said in horror.

Astor replied with a nod, then he threw his bow over his shoulder and hurried out of the barracks with his still-sheathed sword in hand. "Take care, my love."

"You too, love." Helena replied as she picked up her staff. The ice-blue crystal shone bright at her touch. It was ready for another fight.

The Northmen come again.

She took one glance around before leaving. A dozen beds lay empty, ten that had not been slept in for weeks.

Sasha and Correll had died together not three days after their graduation; Nahale had fallen holding the Garuda Pass all alone, saving a thousand refugees and being honored with a statue in the city square. Orrin and Calisto were also gone, dying to emberhounds during the last attack. Haley had joined the recon patrol after Orrin died, and Regis was somewhere to the west aiding the evacuation of the lesser villages.

And Keres,...

Helena shook her head at the bittersweet memories and hurried out the door. She could make out Astor running all alone ahead of her, his long gait unmistakable even in the moonlight. She could see members of the other barracks just starting to emerge.

Knowing Astor would take stock of the situation before acting, Helena hurried to the closest group. "Astor believes the Northmen are coming from the ice spider caves."

"I told you it was Gerould's horn." Willa exclaimed before she hurried after Astor.

"But why has it only sounded twice?" Hugh asked as they started to follow Willa. "It should still be sounding so that we can be sure."

Helena felt her heart seize. Hugh was no fool; if Gerould had stopped his horn, either he was already dead, or something was dangerously wrong. "Where would you go if it is a diversion?"

"Easy, the opposite gate." Bennett remarked. "It is the closest one to the palace, after all."

"It would be," Hugh said, "but the refugees are by the Tempest Gate. An agent of the Northmen could have gotten in with them."

"The horn called us to the Cave Gate!" Willa shouted from twenty paces away. "No other horn has sounded a diversion."

"But Hugh has rarely ever been wrong." Dinah replied meekly.

"There's always a first." Vincent said.

"I'm telling you -" Hugh and Willa cried in unison.

"Enough." Helena barked. The others froze their voices and turned to her, even distant Willa. "Willa and I will go to the Cave

Gate; the rest of you will go with Hugh to Tempest. If he's wrong, I will vouch for your actions. If he's right, hold them until we arrive."

"Understood." Vincent replied. "Hold the gate until we can confirm Hugh's suspicions."

"We will." she said. "Signal if they get through Tempest."

"We will." Hugh said, then the party split. Helena quickly caught up to Willa.

"Do you really think Hugh is right?" Willa asked.

"Can we afford for him to be right and do nothing?"

Willa had no answer. Everyone has an empty bed these days. Time felt like it was running out.

By the time they reached Cave, the battle was fully committed. Somehow the gate had been swung open, the fell beasts and their masters trying to force their way through the tight ranks of the guarding infantry. Helena split off and climbed onto a rooftop to get a vantage point.

No sooner had Helena reached the spot than she saw Willa yell her battle cry and use her wind magic to leap over the line and crash into the heart of the Northmen with her axe. Other frontline mages leapt in after her.

Four blasts of lightning then fell from the wall and lit up the area around Willa before the fell beasts could turn. Helena tracked the jagged trails back to their master. Astor was raining down death as fast as he could draw his bow, even shattering several of the ice spiders with his bolts.

Several other ice mages were picking off two or three Northmen or a single emberhound, but there were too many coming through.

Helena channeled her magic into her staff and loosed a blast of ice at the base of the gate. It struck and encased a dozen men in a spiked wall. She loosed several more bolts as she tried to seal off the gate. The fire mages of the Northmen burned against the wall she was building, but other Serenisi saw her plan and together they formed a barrier twenty feet tall.

Satisfied, Helena turned to the battle below. The confident Northmen should have started to panic with their retreat being cut off, but instead they continued to press forward.

Before she could question why, the building beneath her sagged. Barely able to collect her footing, Helena formed an ice bridge to the roof across the lane and hurried over it as the building collapsed into the ground.

Moments later, Northmen and their fell beasts emerged from the hole.

Helena hesitated at the sight, then turned towards the new threat. She only loosed a single blast before a boulder was hurled towards her. She dove to the side as the boulder shattered the place where she had been standing.

Then she rolled too far, slipping off the side of the roof. Helena tried to form a ramp to smooth her fall, but the impact was still jarring.

Northmen were upon her almost immediately. The staff's crystal flashed as she froze those closest to her. Behind her, she could hear the footfalls of the infantry coming to aid her, but for now she fought alone. With a thought, a blade of ice formed over the head of the staff, and she engaged her foes face to face.

The Northmen were the easier foe to fight. Their leather armor wasn't thick enough to stop the edge of her blade. Though many proved to have some skill, the staff gave her the range to either retreat or hit them with an ice blast should the threat call for it.

Ice spiders were feared by almost everyone, but they are more attuned to the element of ice than any creature and will not challenge a force greater than themselves. With her staff in hand, they instinctively avoided her.

The blazehounds that emerged were a different and far deadlier problem. While she had little worry about the weak embers, blazes could resist the ice long enough to sink their teeth into a mage's neck. While several of them took off down the streets, three turned to their masters' plight and charged her as one, the Northmen scrambling out of their way.

Helena exhaled, focusing her mind on the power needed to chill the blazehounds' fire. The first beast closed in, its heat cutting into the frosty aura that began to swirl. It leapt at her with a howl.

She threw her staff like a javelin. It flew through the heart of the hound and stuck out of its back. The hound fell dead beside her.

As the other two howled and charged, she took hold of the head of the staff and pulled it through the hound before she dove away. These two were not so big as the dead hound, but together their heat was like an oven. The ice she formed at their feet turned to water in a matter of moments.

Something stirred behind her. Instinctively she turned and let loose a stream of ice. Four Northmen who had tried to surprise her were caught in the blast.

A snarl was the only thing that saved her from the leaping blazehound's jaws. Helena twisted away, but she was still taken off her feet. Helena felt the heat of the hound beside her, then it gave a yelp of pain. She rolled over and slapped her hand on the ground, sending out a jagged wall of ice that impaled the creature.

Turning to her right, she saw the flames of the final hound hidden behind a tall shadow.

"How ya holding up, love?" Astor asked nonchalantly before his sword bisected the leaping blazehound.

"Still fighting." She replied as she encased another line of Northmen in ice. "How about you?"

"I'm down to two arrows and I saw you get hit. Figured you might need some help."

"I appreciate it." The two weaved around each other, his sword and her staff cutting down their foes while their allies encircled them. Helena heard Willa's battle cry echo again as the Northmen began to despair.

Then they began to rout.

Helena's joy lasted only a moment before a horn echoed into the night. It was from the direction of the Tempest Gate! "Hugh!"

"Go to him." Astor said as he placed himself between her and the Northmen. "I'll finish up here."

Helena smiled, then stepped towards him. Astor heard her footfall and knew her well, and the two shared a quick kiss before she started towards the call of the horn, leaving several opportunistic Northmen either frozen or electrocuted.

She made it to the gate in record time. Even so, the battle seemed over when she got there, with the fell beasts killed and the Northmen rounded up. But there was no sign of Hugh or the others.

"They're inside the palace!" a soldier exclaimed when she asked. "One of the mages got through and they pursued her."

Helena hurried into the palace. The walls were scorched in several places. At the foot of the stairs she found Bennett burned, only recognizing him by his armor. On another flight was Vincent, barely burned but with a massive gash from hip to shoulder. Near the sanctuary she found Hugh with a broken skull.

Then, by the great balcony of the sanctuary, she saw Dinah struggling to get up.

"Dinah!" Helena exclaimed. She took only a few steps towards the healer before a blast of fire struck her. Helena was lifted from her feet and thrown against the far wall.

When her vision cleared, she saw a mage with raven hair and a commanding presence. "Keres?"

"I'm so glad you could join us, Helena." the traitor mocked as she walked over to Dinah. "You don't know how upset I was that Willa wasn't with her squad so that I could kill them all together, but it will be worth it to have you."

"Leave her alone." Helena said coldly. "She never did anything to you."

"That's true," Keres said as she aimed her staff at Dinah, "but you did. Why should I do anything for you?"

A jet of flame crashed against a block of ice.

Keres laughed as she let a fiery aura engulf her. Helena felt her heart skip a beat. Now Keres could summon an aura like hers?

"Freezing Dinah will only keep her alive for so long." Keres chided. "In her condition, I think she'll succumb to the cold in a few minutes. Then you will have killed her."

"ENOUGH!" Helena launched herself at her former friend. The air began to fill with steam as Keres led her deeper into the sanctuary. Helena struck again and again, switching between her martial and magical prowess with all the skill she had learned.

Every strike was denied by her childhood friend.

Even after months apart, Keres knew what she was apt to try.

Nothing had changed since they were little girls, testing their magic against one another and playing games with the boys. Nothing had changed from the time in the academy building their friendly rivalry.

In the end, Keres caught up as she always did.

And yet, Helena knew she couldn't back off, nor could she back down. She was the one who had mastered her aura first even if she was weaker than Keres. She had become the squad leader over Keres. She had been the one to win Astor's heart.

Astor... "You'll never win Astor now." Helena said.

For a moment she wished she had remained silent. Keres' flames surged with her rage. "I won't lose him to the likes of you!" She threw Helena back with a blast of fire, then nearly stumbled over the ice Helena had formed around her feet.

"You don't need my help for that." Helena said as she powered up her aura.

"As cold as you are, I wonder if you can even keep him warm at night." Keres said as they crossed staves again. "Or will he even accept you into his bed?"

Helena didn't respond. Keres didn't deserve her words. The traitor was too far gone now, and Helena channeled her anger into a furious onslaught as Keres kept talking. Helena refused to hear the words.

Then Keres missed a parry. She lay wide open to a slash from the icy blade. Helena started the strike.

And hesitated.

Keres took advantage and threw her back with a burst of flame that even seemed to consume and extinguish the fiery aura around her. "You think I would accept your mercy?"

Before Helena could rise, another blast struck. Then another.

Then another.

"What's the matter?" Keres called. "Am I too hot for you, ice queen?"

A quiet twang sounded behind her. Keres' eyes snapped to the sound, then her hand caught the arrow loosed at her. Helena saw the small, jagged sparks encircling it and fell back to the ground.

She felt the shockwave of the explosion, and when she looked up Keres was staggering to her feet, her eyes wild with malice and twisted enjoyment.

"Well, if it isn't Astor. I knew you would co-..." Somehow Keres' eyes grew even darker.

Helena turned to Astor, and her heart leapt as she saw Dinah huddled next to him. "You're okay!"

"How dare you, Astor?!" Keres stormed, her body once again in flames. "You had to know it was me! Why would you save her instead of coming to save Helena?"

"I believe in Helena." Astor replied coldly as lightning began to course around his bow, the arrow ready to fly. "And I trusted your jealousy. You wouldn't just kill her at once."

Keres' eye twitched. Then she grinned wickedly. "If you know me so well, then why did Vincent and Hugh and Bennett have to die? Did you want to get rid of them, too?"

Astor didn't reply. Instead, he lowered his draw, his finger tapping the shaft twice as he did so. Helena began to channel her magic at Astor's signal. He continued to glare at their fallen friend. "I didn't think you could be so weak-minded."

"I was always the strongest of us. She will understand that."

"You've let your desires consume you."

"And I am the greatest of us because of it. Can't you see that?"

There was silence for a moment. Helena saw a battle warring on Astor's face. Then he said, almost with no emotion, "I hate you."

Keres' fires went out, and even Helena was shocked by the words. "You can't mean that." Keres said meekly.

"Look what you've become." Astor said in that same tone. "You may be a master of fire, but your heart is as cold as ice."

Helena watched as tears began to well up in Keres' eyes. It pained her, even after all her friend had done. No attack she could unleash could have hurt Keres so much.

Then the flames started to light in the fire mage's eyes again.

"NOW!" Astor commanded.

Helena slapped the ground, a trail of ice lancing out to encase Keres' legs. Keres' gaze turned to them, and Astor's last arrow struck her with a shower of lightning. She let out a cry as the energy tore through her, then she slumped over.

It was over.

"Dinah, try to stabilize her." Astor said gently.

Helena turned to them and saw the hesitance in Dinah's eyes. She wasn't the only one in the room who wasn't sure what to think, but Dinah finally nodded and shuffled over to where Keres was. Helena and Astor went with her, with Helena manipulating the ice so that Keres was reclined and her limbs entombed.

Sure enough, Astor's arrow had merely struck her shoulder. Dinah set to work tending to the wound.

"Why?" Helena asked.

Astor shook his head. Even his posture revealed how unsure he was. "Despite all she has done, I couldn't aim to kill her."

Helena started to reply, but she held her tongue. She had also hesitated to strike the killing blow. "What now?"

"The Masters will deal with her."

"And then?"

Astor stared into her eyes. "I don't know."

Willa came storming into view, a dozen soldiers with her. When she saw Keres, she almost took the traitor's head off. Helena stopped her, and Astor said, "The Masters will pass judgment on her."

"But she -," Willa started, then cursing under her breath she lowered her axe. "At least let me deliver her to the Masters. For my team's sake."

"Of course." Astor replied. Willa then took Dinah and the soldiers and departed with the icebound and unconscious Keres, leaving Astor and Helena behind.

"I wish there was something we could have done for her." Astor said.

"I know." Helena replied. She then turned to him. "Promise me you won't let me become like her."

Astor gave her a sad grin, then he reached out and held her close. "So long as you do the same for me."

She placed her arms around him as a tear fell onto her. "I will."

"FOR HONOR AND BLOOD"

Contest #75: Start your story with one character making a vow that they never would have made the year before.

"I have called you all here to ready the men for battle. My intention is to sail for Ludune province and aid House Scur against the Kaladun invaders."

Mordecai glanced around the table at each of his lieutenants. On his left the Graecian brothers, Alexios and Mateo, were stunned and turned to each other as if to ask whether they had heard correctly. Beside them, Hakeem's eyes fell into the fire so as not to betray the thoughts behind them.

Across from Mordecai, Ibrahim hid his mouth in his hand. Mordecai had made sure that the Emir's representative was present so that the plans for war would be no surprise to the Bloodwolves' patron.

Next to Ibrahim were the Therovingii brothers, Roderic and Baldric. The two greybeards were smiling at the task ahead. Politics weren't their concern; they only cared about having tales of valor for both this life and the afterlife.

Only Altair, seated as always at Mordecai's right hand, displayed no reaction.

The only murmurs were from those standing behind and around the table. Most were the junior officers in the mercenary company, but a few were of the Caletan contingent of his holdings.

Baldric spoke first, rising to his feet as he did so. "I can tell this council that we've been spoiling for a good fight. Ever since we took Palembo, we've faced nothing more than the odd corsair fleet or bandit company. We may be living like kings, but the men are getting soft while the Emir's enemies cower. Much more of this life and we'll be an easy meal for whatever wolf tries to take our place."

"While I agree with Baldric, what of your exile, Cedarsteel?" Mateo said as he rose in challenge. "We have no fear of crossing the borders of Convallis under your banner, but any lord there could put you to death without so much as a thought!"

"I'm sure he's already considered this." Altair's low, meticulous voice countered. He remained seated, having said all that he needed to. The old hawk rarely spoke during such expedition councils as he usually knew beforehand what Mordecai was planning and had a habit of giving the last word. To hear him speak so early put everyone to silence, and both Mateo and Baldric returned to their seats.

With no further words coming from his lieutenants, Mordecai rose from his place at the head of the table. "I am grateful for both your loyalty and your concern, Mateo, and I am in agreement with Baldric that the men need a reminder of why we are paid so well."

Mordecai paused, piecing together his words as best he could. "However, I must tell you that if we do march, this may be the last time that I lead you."

"Why?" Hakeem demanded.

Mordecai could feel the air leave the room. Even Altair, who had known what he was planning, betrayed sorrow at the announcement.

Mordecai couldn't blame them. He had led them to glory and gold for five years, after having proven for two years why he was among the greatest mercenaries fighting along the Great Elysian Sea under Ulysses Redmane, the Bloodwolves' charismatic founder and former commander. They had gone from a minor free company to the chief retainer of Mustafa Pasha, Inaria's most prominent Emir, and they held the Pine Islands and its cities under their direct control.

Mordecai himself had more power and influence than his ancestors had ever wielded, and they were never unknown members of the Convallian court.

In truth, without being banished for killing the king's cousin, Mordecai would never have become who he was today. He'd be a naive nobleman with heady ideals and no knowledge of how the world worked. The peaceful duels of tournaments had been replaced by life-or-death struggles across a hundred battlefields, the orderly sailing of the Great Channel scorned by the survival against the cliffs and tides of a dozen coasts.

He was almost unrecognizable from what he had once seemed destined to be, but home had come calling. "Because I no longer wish to be a mercenary. I wish to have my own lands again, and to find a wife from among my own people."

Hakeem nodded. He, among all the others, would understand this desire, having also been exiled for the misdeeds of his youth and longing to see his desert home again, and the love he had been forced to leave behind.

From the poems Hakeem wrote, Mordecai wished that they could go to the faraway kingdoms and help him find his redemption there. The crossroads of civilizations; the confluence of all the world's cultures, and the one thing Hakeem most desired and would likely never get to see again.

Roderic, meanwhile, scoffed in his usual manner. "As if you have no opportunities here to find a wife." He turned to Altair. "The problem with noble blood is that it doesn't like to be mixed."

The room chuckled at the sentiment, then Roderic continued. "And you, as a fourth son, don't have the advantage of gaining the lion's share of your father's estates. You've carved out a realm for yourself here, much less for the rest of us. What more do you need?"

"Forgiveness." Mordecai surprised himself with how quickly the word came out, but he took advantage of the surprise it afforded. "You are right that we have our own place here. What we have been able to accomplish would be sufficient for many men. But most of you can also return to your people and be welcomed with open arms. I cannot, nor can Hakeem. By coming to my people's aid in their time of trial, they may find a place to forgive what I did."

Several started to speak, but Hakeem leapt to his feet. "Cai, I would not hesitate to follow you into any fight. But I cannot allow you to surrender your post."

"And why is that?" Mordecai asked. He had thought that surely Hakeem would take his side in the argument.

"Roderic speaks true; you will not find a better land nor people than you have now. Having the freedom to go home, and to have someone to remember home by, is one thing. But you are as much a family to us as our own blood relatives. You have sacrificed and bled for us just as much as we have for you."

Hakeem then gave an uncharacteristic bow to Mordecai. "If you wish not to be our captain, then I ask that you be our lord."

Instinctively Mordecai turned to Altair. The old man's eyes were twinkling. Of the rest, only the two Greacians showed any surprise.

Mordecai chuckled and looked to Ibrahim. "I never expected a coup like this. I would assume that the Emir was made aware of my men's plans?"

Ibrahim nodded. "If you will accept Mustafa Pasha's friendship and continue your agreements with him, he is willing to cede the islands to you. After all, you and Ulysses were the only ones to conquer them in centuries. His Eminence would rather not tempt that fate if it could be helped."

Pride formed a smile on Mordecai's face. He had never planned to hold such lands as these, only maybe to receive a small holding upon his father's passing.

He looked around the room again. These men accepted him despite his past and reminded him of why this company had become family to him.

Mordecai turned to Hakeem and gave him a respectful bow. "I'd be a fool to not accept this coup. You have my word; when our march is ended, I will return with you and claim this as my domain."

Hakeem returned the gesture. "Then I will go with you. You have my blade, brother."

"And mine, brother." Alexios said, actually drawing his blade to emphasize the point. The other lieutenants and officers quickly followed.

Roderic and Altair were the last by only a few moments, their proud faces revealing their true feelings about Mordecai's choice.

For perhaps one final time, the whole of the Bloodwolves' mercenary council was behind him.

"Inform the men that we will sail for the Monastan coast in three days." Mordecai commanded. "Ludune province is a week's march inland once we reach those shores. This will not primarily be an expedition for gold, so any man who does not wish to journey will be allowed to stay behind. The spoils will be distributed as normal."

"Many might take that as an excuse to not venture forth." Baldric remarked.

He had considered this possibility. The normal practice of their company stated that those who remained behind in the cities would still receive a quarter portion of the spoils. Ulysses had instituted the practice from the onset of the Bloodwolves so that those who stayed with the supplies didn't lose out, and Mordecai had expanded its scope with the acquisition of the islands.

Mordecai nodded. "I am aware, but this being an expedition begun without a client, I cannot promise much."

"Should we send word on ahead," Mateo asked, "to see if any incentive can be found?"

"No." he replied. "I am not loved back home, and we would likely be rejected outright."

Mateo bowed respectfully at the reply, then grinned. "I suppose it is hard to refuse help when it appears at your threshold."

The council chuckled at this, as did many others in the room. They had used the same tactic numerous times on lesser campaigns, for it provided them with a substantial bargaining position.

"However," Mordecai said slyly, "I harbor no love for Monasta, and to my knowledge they have remained defiant of the Emir's recent tribute demands. Monasta's treasures will be ours for the taking the moment we make landfall."

Everyone cheered at this. Mordecai let a smile slip through as he waited for the cheers to die down, then he dismissed them with the free company's war cry. "For Honor and Blood!"

"For Honor and Blood!"

After the men had left, he went to his quarters and stood on the balcony overlooking the harbor. It was a star filled night, and the moon was full in the sky. There wasn't a cloud to be seen all the way to the horizon.

Below the heavens, the bustling port was lit and lively. Traders were sailing in from up and down the ocean coasts and from the rest of the Great Elysian Sea to the east. His private fleet swung gently at anchor, a fleet that had carried them once to the very walls of the ancient capital of the old Empire. The docks were lined with goods from all corners of the two great continents, and even some luxuries from the lands far to the east.

His gaze shifted further to Caleta herself, the city he had once conquered with Ulysses and then years later had been given as a gift from the Emir.

When he and Ulysses had taken the city, he had insisted upon sparing the citizens and the garrison. That had caused some tension with the Emir at the time, but it had also earned him the gratitude of the islands.

Then, after the Bloodwolves had been expelled from their base on Kyrnos, they returned to the islands to settle the revolts. The Emir, grateful that the islands were no longer in revolt, gave Mordecai the islands as their new base. Today, it was as much a home as Kyrnos had ever been.

Mordecai sighed as he gazed upon the jewel of his mercenary kingdom. His men were not wrong to question if this should be enough. For two and a half years, the city had been enough. His men had been enough.

Convallis's nearest coast was thousands of leagues away around the Inarian Peninsula, barely even within raiding distance if he was ever so inclined.

What was Convallis that he should care about its affairs anymore?

He reached inside the fold of his robes and pulled out the letters. They had arrived just days apart, the last merely four dawns prior. He knew their contents without having to read them anymore.

The first was from his older brother Geoffrey, the crusader whom Mordecai hadn't heard from since the start of his exile, imploring him to return home as Geoffrey himself was.

The second was from the castellan of his father's keep, one of the few who had believed Mordecai's tale, informing him that Mordecai's sister Brigid, who had been captured early in the invasion, had died during an attempt to lift the occupation of Trapain Kolis.

The last was from his mother. She'd written to tell him that the knights of House Cedarsteel had been crushed in battle, and though his father and oldest brother had survived, Kaladun was threatening to march on the castle.

Thinking of Brigid's death brought fresh tears to his eyes. She'd only been nine when Mordecai was banished. She had so much more to live for. Now she was gone, and soon the rest of his family might be.

The Scur family held the lands closest to Caleta, inland from the Monastan coast. They were faced with the brunt of the Kaladun offensive in the south, and from the traders in port Mordecai knew that they were holding strong for now. The king was fighting in the north, where the great cities of Convallis lay.

The Cedarsteel family lands were just south of where the northern fighting was.

Geoffrey would come from the north, with any brothers of his creed that might join him since the holy war against the Northmen had died down. Others might join Kaladun, as the various knightly orders were not unified beyond their creeds. Many felt a longing to fight for home just as Mordecai did, and Kaladun was among the largest of the crusading contingents.

Mordecai's plan was simple. Monasta was one of Kaladun's favored vassals as a buffer with the Inarian emirs, and some pillaging would please Mordecai's men on the way in as well as threaten his enemy's rear. He had no doubt that afterwards he'd join up with the cunning Scurs and together they would drive off Kaladun's southern force.

If he could manage to drive it east instead of north, his men would act as a wedge between the two forces, and Kaladun's king would need to consider whether he wanted to continue driving towards Convallis's heart or move to secure his own flank.

Either way, Mordecai would fight for Convallis.

If the king allowed for it.

He tried to push the doubt from his mind, but it remained. It always remained.

Mordecai knew in his heart that he would always be responsible for Lord Aston's death. If he hadn't been such a rival to him, if they hadn't already dueled once at the young age of thirteen because of a slight, if Mordecai had been the winner of said duel, maybe then it would have been different.

He could still remember the dagger in his hand, his terror when he finally recognized Aston's face in the moonlight.

A true accident that few could ever see as such, even among his own family.

Mordecai clenched his fists. Maybe it wouldn't change anything, but his people were in danger. His family were being killed. He had an army that could aid them, an army feared by many and who had just shown how strong their loyalty to him was. Exile had gifted him a chance to at least try and find redemption in the eyes of his people.

In the eyes of his father.

In his own eyes.

"For Honor and Blood." he whispered.

"ON THE WINGS OF THE BLIZZARD"

Contest #77: Start your story with someone looking out at the snow, and end it with them stepping tentatively onto a frozen surface.

It was all quiet when I opened my eyes and rolled out of bed with a smile. The howling blizzard that had raged for four days had finally passed. Now I could get back to work.

When I opened the window to the cabin, I saw that sunrise was a few minutes yet, her red sunbeams cutting through the fleeing body of the storm.

All around the world was white. The boughs of the evergreens were laden with snow nearly to their breaking point, with jagged scars on several trees where the branches had already given up the fight.

My eyes tracked to one great pine in particular. The snow was just below the blue ring I'd painted on it. That meant the snow was upwards of five feet deep.

I laughed to myself. It was well that I had made for the valley cabin when I'd first felt the cold bite in the air. I'd only just beat the storm by a few hours.

From across the clearing, I heard a whinny. Frost was also awake and ready to get out.

I quickly put on my winter clothes and trekked over to the barn. I fed Frost and then took some wood from the pile back into the cabin. The embers of last night's fire caught quickly, and after a brief trip to the underground storeroom, I had a meal of bacon and potatoes cooking on the stove.

This would be the routine for the coming months, especially if the storms were anything like last year. I'd been caught up high during that first storm and had lived out of the mountain cabin in a miserable state. On the one hand, the thirty feet of snow had insulated the cabin quite nicely once I'd made a hole for the chimney, and I was pleased to learn that I had built the cabin quite strong indeed.

On the other hand, getting anything in the way of further supplies had been a challenge I'd rather not try again.

"This would be the fourth winter, wouldn't it?" I asked myself, making sure that I could in fact still talk clearly. I'd found after a winter of having no one to speak to that I tended to develop quite the enunciation issue once the snows cleared and the mountain men descended back to civilization.

It was indeed the fourth winter I'd settled in for since I'd arrived in the Ruby Mountains, and the fifth since my arrival in this world. I had no understanding of what forces conspired to send me here, nor how to get myself back. While I was fortunate that most people did speak my language in one accent or another, the maps were not of Earth, nor was the history.

It was a riddle I'd given up on when I'd come west, though I still thought of home often enough. I'd come over into this world towards the tail end of 2020, but what had happened back home since then?

I laughed to myself as I took the sizzling meal off the stove. Home was a road frozen in time, and I had no idea where the road started.

I prayed over my food, then planned my day as I ate. It would be wise to see if the lake had frozen thick in the storm or not, as ice fishing would supplement my stores. Thin ice would mean I'd have to wait for the next storm to be confident of not slipping through.

It'd also be good to check on the condition of the passes, though if there was already five feet here, Walker Pass was surely closed up.

"Maybe I should check on Ol' Walk." I vocalized. "See how the beavers are doing this year."

James Walker had been my mentor the first year I'd been in the Rubies. Walk, as he let his friends call him, was an expert trapper that specialized in the beaver trade, but could catch anything you were willing to pay him for. One could say he was the master of the mountain men in these parts, and aside from Red Chapman or Julius Grant, you'd likely get no argument.

Those two were masters in their own right, and if there was a fight I'd rather have them on my side than not, but they lacked Walk's natural charisma. Red and Julius were the type of mountain men an Easterner would avoid; Walk was the type they loved to romanticize about in their dime novels.

Walk had taught me the trapper's trade well enough. Even now I had a stack of furs from the mountain cabin that I'd hoped to get into town before the winter fell, but my coin purse and my storeroom were full enough as it was, and the furs would still be good when the snow cleared.

In the back of my mind, I wished to get to the stock exchange in Newhaven to check on those mining shares I'd purchased, but that was a relatively small position, and I'd left instructions with Mr. Abbot about how to handle the shares. He was about as honest a bookkeeper as one could hope for. If nothing else, both Walk and Red swore by him.

With the food devoured, I gathered some jerked meat and filled my canteen to put in my pack, then loaded my rifle and revolver, holstering the latter next to my hunting knife. Back in the barn I saddled Frost, making sure to add two blankets and some firewood in case the mountains decided to storm unexpectedly.

Once she was saddled and my rifle was secured in its saddle scabbard, we started off into the snowbound woods.

A couple hours later, I was nearing the lake when I spotted tracks to my left. I thought little of them at first and let Frost keep on her course. Then they turned towards us and crossed ahead of us.

Only when we were about to go over them did they truly seize my attention. The hair on my neck stood up as I dismounted and studied them. They were human, and by the snow infill, they were made last night.

That meant only one thing. Someone had been out in that blizzard, and they likely needed help. I quickly got back on Frost and began to follow the footprints.

Three miles further on, I spotted a second trail merging with the first. This one had no infill, making the snow tiger's prints clear. I urged Frost to go as fast as she could in the thick snow. Now it was a race not only against the elements, but also against nature's predators.

As Frost's hooves crunched through the snow, I pulled out my rifle. Snow tigers were as ornery as any cougar back on Earth, and as vicious as a mad mama grizzly. Even Walk took special care to avoid them if he saw their tracks. If I were to shoot, I wanted to do so at a fair range, and if I didn't drop it with the first shot and it dipped out of sight, the entire ride home would be a paranoid one.

The problem was that fair range. My effective range was four hundred and fifty yards if I were shooting at a buck. Red once said that he hit a snow tiger at two hundred yards with the same model of rifle and the cat still got away. Knowing this, I'd likely need to get within one hundred yards to land a disabling shot.

If the rifle misfired, the pistol's effective range was closer still.

Another problem was accuracy. While between the two guns I had thirteen shots loaded, I was not very accustomed to firing from horseback, and Frost had a tendency to jump at the sound of gunfire. Most likely I would get one good shot, then it'd be a scramble to see if whoever I was following was still alive before riding off.

Then again, a snow tiger was faster than Frost even in an open field. I'd seen a snow tiger run down an elk once, two harvests back. It was the only time I'd ever seen the beast alive, and I'd viewed it with the mixture of wonder and terror one has when they see an apex predator in its natural environment. If I kept riding forward, this would most likely become a situation of kill or be killed.

I saw the stripes from around the dead pine a moment before I heard the roar. It was several hundred yards off, but my veins froze. Walk had told me that the roar meant one of two things; either the cat was protecting his territory, or it was signaling the kill. The snow tiger was turned away from me, and beyond him I saw a huddled form beside a tree.

I fired, making sure I wouldn't hit the person. Frost jumped and the bullet missed, but the shot got the tiger's attention. It turned and glared with yellow eyes, and as I aimed and fired a second shot the cat slipped behind the trees, though I swore that I saw the hide at the base of its tail jump.

If that bullet had hit, the cat made no acknowledgement of it.

I urged Frost to loop towards the person, keeping my eyes trained for the cat. Frost was a good horse, and she went along the most open path she could find. I'd glance forward every so often to see where she was going, then turn back, hoping to spot the stripes.

For now, it remained hidden, which terrified me to no end.

Even so, the cat let us reach the young lady we all were tracking. I immediately took her as a city girl, though she was dressed like a cattle hand. Her leather jacket had some tears in it, as did her denims that were wholly unsuited for the snowy weather she'd been in. There was no fade from the sun present on her hat, and her belt buckle was too shiny. At least she had a good pair of riding boots on. They were in fact the only things she had that appeared to be worn in.

"You alright, miss."

"Better than I could be." she said hoarsely as I dismounted. "If you hadn't come, I -"

I cut her off. "Don't thank me yet. Snow tigers aren't known to give up easily. We need to get away from here."

She looked at me with wide eyes. I couldn't decide if confusion or fear was the dominant force behind them. She started to say something, then bit her tongue and dropped her eyes.

"I assume you can ride?" I asked as I pulled a blanket from my pack and put it around her.

She nodded. "I can."

"Good." I extended my hand and helped her to her feet. Her movements were pained. She needed a fire and a good meal in her, but we were hours from that at any rate. "You'll ride while I walk."

Her eyes went wide again. "What about the cat?"

"I want both hands free to use my rifle." I drew my pistol and handed it to her. "Keep your eyes open for it. It won't do much against the cat's hide, but the noise will disorient it."

"And what will you do?" she asked as I helped her onto Frost.

I didn't answer immediately as I tried to decide whether to reload a new tube of ammo or stick with the remaining five shots I had. I finally chose to just go, as reloading would give the cat a golden opportunity. Even if it attacked, I likely wouldn't get to fire more than five times.

Next time I'm in Newhaven, I'll go to the armory and demand someone invent the box magazine. "I'll lead the horse. We'll follow my trail back to the cabin and hope that the cat decides on some easier prey."

After a moment to scan for the cat, I led Frost back towards home. It dawned on me that I hadn't asked the lady's name, but that could wait until we were safe.

We reached the convergence point in a half hour, then the place where her tracks first crossed mine an hour and a half beyond that. At this rate, we might reach the cabin by nightfall with the ever-shortening winter days.

There was still no sign of the cat, but I had that sixth sense of being watched.

The lady was quiet the entire time, and the times I looked back I was encouraged to see that she did hold the pistol properly, her finger not on the trigger but near enough to fire quickly. Her eyes were alert, if also terrified, and the few times we had heard something or Frost had sounded a warning, she was ready.

I'd just opened my mouth to speak with her when Frost whinnied and reared back. The lady managed to stay in the saddle and trained her gun to my left. I turned to see the yellow eyes leaping from its ambush, no more than twenty yards downwind from us.

The snow tiger roared as I raised my rifle to fire. The pistol barked once. I saw the shot impact on the snow tiger's shoulder, then I fired at the cat's head as quickly as I could. The first shot went low and hit the cat's chest, the second seared its cheek as the tiger seemed to evade, and the third hit right as it lunged.

I dove to the side, but the cat still caught my shoulder and spun me, knocking the rifle from my grasp. I tried to draw my hunting knife as I hit the ground. It wasn't a clean draw, but I came up with the knife in hand.

The cat lay still on the ground. I slowly reached down to pick up the rifle, and even though the cat didn't move I fired another round into it, saving the last in case it came up. A few seconds later I inched closer.

My third bullet had caught it between the eyes.

With a sigh, I sheathed my knife and told the lady, "It's dead."

"Good." she replied, though I still heard terror in her voice. She looked at me apologetically. "Sorry I only fired once. I wasn't expecting a single action."

"No worries, miss." I told her, though the remark piqued my interest. I hadn't yet heard of a dual action gun being produced. "Frost doesn't like gunfire, so you probably only had a single shot."

She smiled sheepishly, and I turned back to the snow tiger. It was easily ten feet from nose to the base of its tail, and the tail was at least three feet more. Upon further examination, I decided that I wanted the hide, if for nothing more than bragging rights when the snow melted.

The lady dismounted to watch me tie up the cat, and even helped me pick up the cat to slide the rope under, though her arms trembled at the weight.

Once this was done, I secured the rope to Frost's saddle, then took some of the jerky and the canteen and handed it to the lady. She thanked me, and after she'd eaten, we mounted and rode off.

The snow tiger's corpse glided over the snow as we headed home, now in an awkward sort of silence. I'd never been the best at small talk, especially with women, and she was understandably still in some state of shock.

She broke the silence when she saw my cabin. "Is that yours?"

"Built it myself." I said proudly. "Chimney's still smoking, so we should be warm."

She sighed. "That sounds great."

We rode up to the barn, and after dismounting I helped her down. I'd helped enough women down from the wagon trains that this at least was natural. Once I'd stabled Frost, I led her inside.

Her... "Pardon me, but I realize I never asked for your name."

She had already started assessing every detail of the cabin, so when she turned with a smile, I figured I'd kept the place well enough. "Sierra. Sierra Kipling. What's yours."

"Jean Daniel. Tremblay." I replied, pronouncing 'Jean' as '*zhon*'. My mother's French heritage made my name unique, especially here. But now that we were on a first name basis, my inquisitive side had questions. "What brings you out here without proper clothing? That blizzard was raging for a good four days before today."

Sierra's brow furrowed. "It had only just started snowing last night."

Now I was confused, but I returned to the first question hoping that it would clear up a few things. "Those aren't proper clothes for snow regardless."

"I hadn't expected the mustang to slide off the road." she replied. "I'd thought that town was only a few miles away."

Why were you riding in this weather? I thought, but I pressed on. "Sorry to hear that, Miss Sierra, but the nearest town is ten miles through a pass that's likely closed off due to the blizzard."

Her jaw dropped. "I can't be that far into the woods. I hadn't driven that long."

"What way did you take?" I asked.

"Highway 26." Sierra replied.

My head tilted involuntarily in response. Numbered roads were a city thing; out here everything was trails and passes.

Numbered highways..! Suddenly it clicked what her Mustang really was.

Sierra had to be from Earth, like I was!

I leaned forward, and hesitated. What if she wasn't, and I was about to sound like a lune again? Yet what if she said yes? What if we could find the way home? Did that frozen road exist nearby? Was meeting her the first step down it?

You might never get another opportunity to take that step.

"You're from Earth, aren't you?"

"IN THE WAKE OF THE BLIZZARD"

Contest #77: Set your story in a remote winter cabin without electricity, internet, or phone service.

"You're from Earth, aren't you?"

Jean Daniel's question left me speechless. I'd nearly blurted out "Of course," but just as he had seemed to have a lightbulb moment a few seconds ago, I was having one now. The mountains and trees had never looked right today. Jean Daniel's guns were basically relics compared to those back home Though, to be fair, they had killed the snow tiger.

Heck, that name alone should have told me that there was something wrong; I had just been too frightened to think about it.

Suddenly Jean Daniel started to laugh. "That's what my face must have looked like when I first realized it, too." He said as he sat down into a chair.

He's from Earth? I thought as I sat down. "How'd we end up here?"

His expression turned. "I'd hoped that you would shed some light on that. I woke up here five years ago."

"Five years?!"

He nodded. "Well, not here specifically. I woke up on a ship bound for Kingston and stayed there the first winter, then I came out west the next summer and have been mostly in this area ever since."

Five years. I couldn't believe being out here for that long.

Then again, he had clearly done well for himself. The cabin and the barn looked well-built and had that rustic charm I'd always loved. And he could clearly handle a gun and wasn't afraid of the local predators. "Do you know anything about what brought you here?"

He shook his head. "I spent almost a year searching for answers before I left Kingston. Never caught so much as a whiff."

There was a twinkle in his eye. I'd been around enough young men to know that he was scheming something. "What are you thinking?"

"If we follow your trail back, we may find an answer."

My heart leapt in my throat, but I glanced at the shuttered windows and saw that the light behind them was dim.

He seemed to recognize my thoughts. "We would need to follow your tracks tomorrow. I wouldn't expect any more snow tigers, but this world does have plenty of wolves."

I felt a twinge of fear. I'd be alone all night with this stranger. Sure, he'd saved my life, but what could I do if he were like some of the guys I knew at college? There was no one to stop him.

"Don't worry. I can sleep in the barn with Frost if that would make you feel better about this." He said with a smile. "I still remember my first day. I was lucky to convince the sailors that I wasn't a stowaway, or it would not have been a pleasant experience. They made sure to tell me the stories afterwards."

"What kind of ship was it?" I asked, relieved that Jean Daniel had some decency to him.

"A two-masted sloop. She'd been a blockade runner during the last war and was now a smuggler's ship. You can imagine the master's surprise and disdain when I seemingly smuggled myself aboard his ship."

I chuckled. "That would be startling. What did you do before the ship?"

He looked to the ceiling, as though trying to recall those memories. "Nothing really of note. I had graduated college and was working a desk job at an engineering firm. Needed to get out one night and fell asleep stargazing. I woke up on the ship."

I couldn't withhold a laugh.

"What?"

"I never would have guessed you for an engineer. Though," I said as I glanced around the cabin, "that would explain your design style. Very efficient layout. I'm guessing this place is built like a fort."

His face turned a little red. Clearly, he wasn't used to getting a compliment from a girl. Typical of the few engineering students I'd met. "Well, the place hasn't given me any problems. My cabin higher up survived a thirty-foot snowfall last year, but that place has a much steeper roof pitch."

"Nerd." I teased, and he went a little redder.

"What were you back home?" he asked.

I sighed. "I'm still in college, majoring in film design. Lived in LA my whole life, though I have cousins up in Oregon that I love visiting. I won the college surfing competition a few months ago, almost won the beach volleyball tournament after that. Had plans to go to Hawaii with some friends after the semester finished."

"26 doesn't run through California. Guessing you were up with your cousins when you went off the road, right?"

Wow, he remembered that? "I was. My cousin Gwen had a riding exposition, and I dressed up for the occasion."

"They the ones that taught you to ride and shoot?"

I breathed a laugh. "You're figuring me out pretty quick."

Jean Daniel smiled. "Engineers like patterns."

"So it would seem. Anything else?"

"Guessing you still live with your parents?"

"Do you know how expensive college is?" I shot back. For some reason, that question stung. All he had to do was raise his eyebrows, and I realized my mistake. "Sorry, of course you do."

"That's alright. I stayed home the first couple years, myself. Good financial choice, but I had a much better time once I moved out."

"Then why'd you ask?"

Jean Daniel held his tongue for a moment. "Forgive my saying so, but you come across as very sheltered."

"And why-" I stopped myself before I went any further. My gaze turned to one of the cabin walls. If he had once been sheltered in addition to being an engineer, he no longer was. "I guess trying to walk out of a snowstorm would seem a bit foolish to you."

"You're not the only fool who's tried." he remarked, then he smiled. "Though you might be the prettiest."

I felt my cheeks blush, and his went a couple shades redder as well. I played coy. "Isn't it a bit soon to say that, cowboy?"

"Mountain man, Miss Sierra, and that was revenge for earlier." He stood up and went to the cupboard. "I don't have much in the way of variety, but I'm mighty hungry. You good with meat and potatoes," he turned back towards me, "or are you more the herbivore type?"

I feigned offence. "I may be a California surfer girl, but I'll eat anything you put in front of me."

"Good to hear." Jean Daniel set down a jug and two wooden mugs on the table, then he put a skillet and a pot on the stove. He then opened an unseen trapdoor and disappeared, coming back a minute later with a few potatoes and two thick steaks. Jean Daniel set these in the skillet and took the pot to the window. He opened the shutter, scooped up some snow, and returned it to the stove.

At least the water will be clean, I thought.

"Miss Sierra, can I ask something of you?"

"What?" I replied, wondering if he'd want me to peel the potatoes or something.

"Could you light the lanterns before it gets too dark? I tend to forget until after sunset."

"Sure." I replied. He picked up a thin piece of kindling and lit its end before handing it to me. The lanterns were easy enough to see and soon the main room of the cabin was fully lit. However, while I discovered that he had both a bedroom and a study through the two doors on one side, the only other door I saw was the entrance. "Jean Daniel, where is the bathroom?"

He laughed. "Through the left door, around the bookcases."

I proceeded into the study, lighting the lantern on the way. There must have been a hundred books on those shelves, but I was reminded of the time period when I opened the little door to see a box with a seat.

Returning to the main room a bit later, I saw Jean Daniel smirk. "It's better than most cabins you'll find out here, but hopefully you won't need to get used to that."

"I agree." I replied as I eyed the food. He was whipping the potatoes with a fork and the meat was looking delicious. Not more than a minute later he cut one open and asked me if the color was right.

"It's less pink than I would like," I replied sheepishly, "but it isn't black."

With that we sat down to eat, after Jean remembered to get some more silverware. He bowed his head in silent prayer, and reassured I did the same. From the first bite I admitted,

"A bit plain, but it tastes very good. My compliments to the chef."

Jean Daniel smiled. "I'll forward them to him."

I smiled, then tried the cider from the jug. The meal passed slowly as we talked. First I asked Jean Daniel about this world, then he began asking about me and Earth.

We were almost done when he lifted the jug and realized I had consumed most of it. "I don't want to be accused of getting you drunk the first night I met you." he said, with more than a little worry in his voice.

"I've had stronger drinks." I replied defiantly, but neither that nor any other argument worked to get any more of the sweet nectar. It was probably for the best, because within half an hour I was feeling well off my rocker. All that Jean Daniel did was laugh a bit and lead me to the study. He left and came back with several furs that he laid on the floor, and soon I buried myself in them and was out like a light.

I woke up with a start, but I quickly found that everything was where it was supposed to be. Still in a bit of a daze, I walked into the main room.

The sun was well into morning, and the only sign that Jean Daniel was awake was what looked like a muffin on the table. Taking that it was for me, I tried it. His baking skills still needed some work, but it was alright.

I wandered out into the snow. Jean Daniel was out in the barn, having just finished skinning the snow tiger. "Finally awake?" he asked, spying me from the corner of his eye.

"Yeah. Guess that cider was stronger than I thought."

He laughed. "If you like that stuff, you should try Red Chapman's. His will knock an unsuspecting man flat." He touched up a few places on the hide, then he turned towards Frost. "Are you ready to seek some answers?"

It took a moment to realize he was speaking to me. "Of course."

Jean Daniel took the reins and led Frost out of the barn. "If we do find a way home, it will be interesting to see what has changed."

"Well, you missed quite the presidency." I told him, thinking of the insanity both sides had shown during the Trump presidency.

"Wow. I wouldn't have thought Biden would upstage Trump's four years."

"Biden's inauguration is this week." I replied before thinking about what he said.

He looked at me confused. "Biden hasn't taken office yet?"

I had finally caught what Jean Daniel had said. "No, and he did defeat Trump."

"I was still on Earth when he did." came the reply.

We stood there in silence for a minute, each trying to make sense of what the other was saying. Frost, while patient at first, finally got fed up with waiting and reared up slightly. I nearly tripped over myself when she did, and Jean Daniel verbally rebuked her.

"What does this mean?" I asked.

"Well, it could mean one of two things." Jean Daniel said as his eyes dipped in thought, for the first time sounding like an engineer. "The first is that we were dropped randomly into this world's timeline, meaning that if we go back, we may not be in the right year at all. We could be going to the Old West for all we know, and even if we go through one after the other, we may end up in vastly different places."

I didn't like that possibility. "And the other?"

"The other is that time on Earth is dilated relative to this world. However, the span is roughly a half year here for every week on Earth. I don't think gravity and relativity can explain that jump given the Sun's density, but I may be wrong. In that case, we are likely in a parallel dimension with a different relativity but similar natural laws." He returned his gaze to me and must have seen my smirk. "What?"

"I believe you were an engineer now." I replied with a head tilt. "So, what does that mean for us?"

"Well, if the second one, very little for you. For me, I'll have lived five years in ten weeks, and I don't know how I feel about that."

I didn't reply; I didn't know how to reply to that.

After a few moments though, he grinned. "We'll cross that bridge when we get to it. For now, let's see if we can even get home."

Frost moved much faster through the snow today than she had yesterday, thanks to not towing the snow tiger. Jean Daniel quickly found my tracks, then we followed them into the forest. It appeared that I hadn't managed to walk that far before crossing Jean Daniel's path, for we soon came to a point where my trail just ended.

Almost like I had literally stepped into this world.

Jean Daniel dismounted, then helped me down.

"What do you make of this?" I asked.

He took a deep breath. "I almost want to just walk back over and see if there is an invisible portal."

"Should I?"

Jean Daniel looked into my eyes, then he glanced at Frost before returning to me. "You first."

I felt a twinge in my chest. "Will you follow?"

A muscle in his face twitched. "I'm not sure yet. I've built quite the life here, but I can practically just go back to my life on Earth as well." He smiled, seemingly to reassure me. "You don't have that dilemma."

"But what if I do?" I wasn't teasing this time, though I wasn't sure why I'd said it that way either. What I did know was that it would be difficult to find someone like him back home, who would face down a snow tiger for me and not take advantage of me.

That, or I was being a hopeless romantic like my mother.

His cheeks went a little red, though not like before. "Isn't it a bit early to speak of such things?"

I laughed. "True, but I think you're a good man, Jean Daniel. Unless you prove me wrong."

Now he laughed. "Now why would I do that?" He held out his hand, and I put mine into it. "We'll step through together."

Smiling, we walked towards the end of the trail. I felt my heart beat faster. This was like some sort of fantasy. It was surreal.

We took the last step.

The forest remained the same.

A moment of disappointment passed, then we broke into laughter. Frost seemed to get the joke and whinnied behind us. "Of course it wouldn't be that easy." Jean Daniel exclaimed.

I was about to reply when I felt my phone buzz. I quickly pulled it out. The phone was almost dead, but it had several notifications, including messages from my family and friends. "I have a signal!"

He hurried to my side. After a few moments, he gently took the phone from my hands and moved it in the air. For a while nothing happened, but at a point just behind my footprint the battery began to drain, and a small light appeared, growing into a tiny ring.

Jean Daniel yanked the phone back before the light grew any bigger.

"What was that?" I asked as he quickly made an X in the snow.

"Send a message about what's happened before your phone dies. We don't have enough energy to open the portal. The blizzard's natural energy must have done it."

"How?"

"Sometimes snowstorms will generate lightning." he said as he looked around, then he pointed. "Look at that tree! That scar is fresh. The bolt must have been enough to open it."

I felt a grin of excitement spread across my face. "So how do we get back? Wait for the next storm?"

"Or create a generator. I know the basic principles, but it will take some time."

"Then why send a message?"

"Because the signal can be traced to here, and then they can try to open it from their side."

"Would they believe me?"

"That's why I said a generator was an option."

I stopped short. We now knew we could get back, and Jean Daniel knew of three ways to do it. I quickly worded a message, showed him to see if it made enough sense, then hit send. The message made it out, but my phone was practically dead. "Should I leave it here for them to trace?"

"You can." he replied. "Not sure how long they'll see it given the time dilation though." He had run a rope between two of the trees so that it passed over the X. He then tied a small strand over that point. "That should tell us where it is, and if the rope breaks the cut strands can be used to find it again."

We stood there for a few moments. I looked at him. "Well, I suppose I will need a place to stay."

He caught my tone. "The study is yours until we get you home."

I smiled at him. "You're going to do this right, aren't you Jean Daniel?"

He smiled. "I hope that doesn't disappoint you, Miss Sierra."

"Not at all." I replied, then we walked back towards Frost.

THE UNFINISHED

TALES

"A FATHER'S LEGACY"

Unsubmitted story for Contest #38.

"Will, your father wasn't just human."

Up until I heard those words, I had lived a normal life. I was getting by in high school without too much bullying, though my social standing was among the lower rungs to say the least.

Ah, a typical teenager's thinking, to immediately jump to social hierarchies when recounting his history. Allow me to start again.

My life until those words was normal, except for the success of my father. After publishing a book about his rebellious teenage years, he had written a series of fantasy books that had taken the world by storm. *Mystical Travels* was based on his supposed adventures in another realm starting from the year before he met my mother, a realm filled with elves and dwarves and magic.

It was written as a narrative history of my father's time in that realm as kings ruled, elves and dwarves and fairies warred for control, dragons appeared and needed to be slain, and dark forces turned friends into foes.

I had grown up with these tales quite literally, as my father included me and my siblings in his tales during periods when his character was back in our reality. That had the unfortunate side effect that some people in school knew more about me than I would like, but to say that the realm didn't fascinate me would be a lie.

I knew all the main characters as if they were old friends, to the point that I could picture their faces and hear their voices. Alwen the Wise, Finadin the Shade, Gwendolyn the Fair Queen; they and more were better known to me than anyone outside of my family. I compared people to them, usually finding the real people to come up short in my estimations.

This was true especially when comparing the girls in my school to Helena, Alwen's granddaughter and my father's goddaughter in the tales. She had been born soon after I was according to the books' timeline.

But I'm going down another tangent again, aren't I?

At any rate, the worlds of my father's books had always been more real to me than our world, and I struggled because of it.

Then one morning, my father was brutally stabbed while on his morning walk. Later that day, while we were still clinging to hope that he would survive, someone broke into our house. Neither perpetrator had been found, and my father was now dead.

I admit that I cried for a week at any mention of him or his beautiful world. I had lost my father and the realm of my escapism in one moment.

While many offered condolences, some had asked if I would take up his place, since I had published a novel about my own realm on my 16th birthday not long before. As much as I would have liked to, I was no writer like my father, and I could only make a mere imitation of that realm.

Today when I came home from school, I found my mother was in the back room with several men. I could only hear their voices in the hallway at first, and I heard Alfwen's name mentioned.

Instantly my mind turned to dark thoughts. *More corporatists or journalists looking to profit from our tragedy.*

My family had suffered them long enough, so I headed in there to tell them to leave. From the entrance I could see that my sisters were also with my mother. I felt my anger growing. *Even my sisters aren't immune to your greed?!*

I rounded the corner of the room, and before I spoke a word in anger, I saw the visitors.

If ever there was clothing to match the elves in *Mystical Travels*, they wore it. The four also had long straight hair and fair skin... and pointed ears.

"I take it you are William?" one of the men said. His voice sounded old and aged, which cut against his more youthful face, but it sounded familiar. I must have looked confused as I pondered it, for the man began to laugh. "Please, sit with us. We have much we would like to tell you."

"Tell me about what?" I had asked, still trying to place that voice.

This was the moment my mother turned to me and said, "Will, your father wasn't just human."

Now, hearing those words should have been confusing. Everything that was going on should have been confusing. A logical person should have asked a thousand questions, chiefly if he had just been dreaming the entire day up until this point of lucid insanity.

But it was at that moment that the voice clicked. It shouldn't have, for I had never met the man. Yet it was the voice I had given him whenever he had counseled my father during his travels. In perhaps the dumbest moment of brilliance I would ever have, I turned to him and asked, "Is that you, Alwen?"

You could have heard a pin drop as everyone exchanged confused gazes between me and Alwen, for he most assuredly was the elven lord. He was the first to break the silence. "My, my. It seems your father was right when he said that you would know me at once."

"His stories? They were all real?"

"Indeed." Alwen replied.

"Will, you must understand," my mother interrupted, but Alwen held up a hand.

"We have come to offer our condolences for your loss," he said, "and we are also here for you."

"Me?" I asked, as any reasonable person might.

"As you've no doubt read, your father was blessed with magic during his time in our realm." one of the other elves explained. "That gift has passed down to all of his children, though we took steps to keep it locked away until you were old enough to use it wisely, so that you might live in this realm without raising suspicion."

"It was also foreseen that one of his children would take his place when he passed." another continued. "It may seem like some morbid irony, but you have come of age just as the torch needs to be passed."

I just stood there listening. On one hand, I was trying to take in the cascade of what was being told to me, and on the other, being overwhelmed by a growing sense of excitement. This sense soon took dominance when I finally found the ability to speak again. "When do we leave?"

"William!" my mother exclaimed. She clearly thought that I was taking this too well.

The elves simply laughed at my remark. There was a twinkle in Alwen's eye. It was just as my father had described when the elf was going to give a riddle. I was already preparing to think about his question when he spoke. "As soon as you open the way."

In a flash I was going to my father's study. It was the one place across all the tales that I had known. Bookshelves along one wall, the desk sitting opposite, the electric fireplace decoration against the far wall that made it seem like something out of an old book.

I went to the bookshelf and reached for my father's favorite book, *Sitka*, pushing it back against the wall.

Nothing.

I tried again.

Still nothing.

I couldn't understand what was wrong. This was how the gateway to Athelion was activated. I'd read about it so many times. It was even up so far that I could never have accidentally pushed the book over and entered the portal, if all the stories were true.

Yet, nothing.

I just stared at the books as they mocked me. Was the riddle as simple as I had first thought? My father had seemingly written many clever characters. If they too were real, surely such a method was not the correct course.

Yet, he had consistently given this as the method in the tales for two decades.

Maybe if I read one of my father's books again, it will help. I thought as I reached for my father's own books. Except, they weren't where they had always been. They were now one shelf down, having swapped their place with the stories of other current fantasy writers.

Curious, I looked at them. There had to be a reason for that. Each tale was in their published order though. There was nothing odd about that.

"Are you stumped as well?"

I jumped as Alwen and the rest entered. For a moment I wanted to tell them that I wasn't, but I also didn't want to lie. The old elf would likely see right through the lie, anyway. "I did what my father would in the tales, but it didn't work. Then I found that the books have been moved."

"Interesting." the elf said cryptically.

The way it came across, this change had been deliberate. "Why did you change them?" I asked.

There was a moment of wonder in the elf's eyes. Even before he said, "It was not I who did this", I knew that it was something that my father had done. He had changed the order, and so recently that I hadn't noticed it before his death.

I had a harrowing realization and turned to Alwen. "My father wasn't killed by a human, was he?"

Alwen's eyes dropped for a moment, telling me all I needed to know. Someone had crossed back over and murdered my father, but he had changed the return sequence beforehand.

As if he had been preparing for this to happen.

Without reply, I turned back to the books. "Did you catch him?"

"The faerie took his own life before we could capture him."

There was a little darkness of rage that took hold in that moment. "When did that happen?"

"After he couldn't get back through the gateway."

It suddenly dawned on me. "This really is the only way between our worlds, isn't it?"

"The only stable way that we know of. Others have appeared and disappeared, but as you know -."

"Even Andulan never succeeded in creating a way to my world." I recalled from the tales as I turned back to the elves. There were stories of the ancient Atlantii who had constructed the old gateways before their downfall. A few of them still lived in a realm they had created, but they had sequestered themselves from the other realms. My father had been gifted a small gateway by the Atlantii in one of his earliest travel.

Since the time of the Atlantii's height, only Andulan had managed to even approach their proficiency in crossing between the realms. "So then, you all are essentially stuck here as well."

Alwen nodded. "The way back has been closed since your father died. He kept many things a secret."

Sighing, I recited one of my father's favorite phrases, "Well, some secrets never left the *Sit-*"

OF COURSE!

I slid over to the end bookcase. The first book he ever wrote was about his voyage aboard his friend's sailing sloop *Sitka,* a mostly biographical tale which had always been mocked for that one fanciful chapter that seemed to spawn all of the *Mystic Travels.* That book was the *Sitka* of the tales.

I chuckled as I reached the bookcase. To no surprise, that story had also been moved from its place. That place was now occupied by a spine I recognized. It was my debut novel. With a smile, I pressed my fingers against the novel and pushed.

The orange swirls of the gateway erupted around me. My sisters squealed in delight while my mother and the elves gasped. I was the only one who made no sound. I was too enthralled to make one. The magic was just as I'd seen it in my mind.

The orange slowly shifted to blue, just as my father described it, then I began to count down.

Three.

Two.

... One.

When the color faded, I knew where I was. The marble fountain with its gold trim sat amid an immaculately groomed garden. The great mansion surrounding us on all sides. And if I could see beyond that, the majestic elven city of Athelion would be sprawling out before me.

I let out my breath with excitement. "We're here."

"We are." Alwen said.

Before he could say anything further, I spied an elf-maiden in the distance. At once I knew who the dark-haired girl was. "That's her, isn't it?"

"Who?" Alwen asked before he followed my eyes. "Ah. Yes, that's Helena."

My mother spoke up. "Will, you only just got here."

"Yes, but I'm to take Dad's place. I should go introduce myself."

She looked at me for a moment. Then a smile broke across her face. "I suppose your father would be happy you are approaching a girl for once."

The retort stung, but not as much as I would have thought. I looked to Alwen, and he nodded his approval. With more confidence than I had ever had, I crossed the garden to Helena.

She saw me at a distance, and after a moment of surprise the elf-maiden started walking towards me as well. We met beneath a blooming tree.

"I'm William, the son of James Gering."

Helena smiled brightly. "I've heard much about you, Will. I'm Helena, the daughter of Branwen and Fuiliel."

"I've heard much of you, too." I replied.

And so started my time of taking up my father's legacy in the magical realms.

"THROUGH THE WORMHOLE"

Unsubmitted story for Contest #44.

Sometimes people wish curiosity would take a back seat. It often leads to some great discoveries and adventures, but it also often leads to great pain and distress.

Only once have I ever felt both ways at once. I was lost in a strange world and without any means by which to get home, cursing the moment that I had wandered off in search of the sound in the caverns and found the wormhole that my father had been chasing for years.

I had heard the theories of what a wormhole might look like many times while growing up. As an intern I sat through meetings while presentations were given, and new variables were discussed. I had seen the initial tests in the collider, the fourth such device in the facility that was built within the cave systems beneath the capital.

After the test staff was pared down and I was hired by a neighboring facility to help develop self-propelled wingsuits, I'd exploited my own knowledge of the caves to sneak in.

That was how I heard the sound as I hurried to catch the start of that day's testing. It was a high-pitched hum, likely beyond the hearing of the older researchers. They probably would have dismissed it as some vibration from the collider's operation.

I almost believed that too, until I turned my head and found that the sound was directional, coming from further on past the corridor I had planned to take.

Curiosity struck, and I followed it to find the pale blue spiral within a small cavern. I stared at it in awe. The theories were right; we could create a wormhole. It was just appearing outside of the collider for some unknown reason.

Looking back, the smart thing would have been to leave and report what I'd found. I would have gotten in severe trouble for having a secret way into the collider, but the discovery surely would have covered over that sin.

However, curiosity took the driver's seat of my thoughts. *What lay on the other side?* I'd wondered, and no amount of common sense could shake that question.

So, without proper gear or anything to survive outside of the cave I was in, I stepped through the wormhole.

The experience was anticlimactic in and of itself. The moment I crossed the event horizon I was on the other side. No weird sensations, no travel through some swirling mist, nothing at all. Like walking through a doorway.

The hillside view I found myself on, though, was breathtaking. The brilliant orange sky with its pink and yellow clouds floating among trees hundreds of feet tall with billowing canopies. Through the trees I saw a wide river, and against its bank was a city which seemed dropped from a faerie tale.

It was amazing, until the sound of the wormhole faded behind me.

When I turned back, it was gone.

I have heard it said that panic kills. That was the moment I fully understood why. For a few minutes I stood there cursing myself out until I finally took a seat and tried to figure out a plan.

That's when a new sound caught my ear. It was the rapid beating of wings, like a hummingbird, but much larger. I spun around to see what animal was about to attack me.

Except, it wasn't an animal.

It was, from all appearances, a human-sized faerie with long red hair, pinkish wings, and a satchel hanging from her shoulder. Her clothing though was barely different from what many girls wore in college, save for the open back to accommodate the wings.

"Don't be frightened." she said as she landed several yards away. "I mean you no harm."

The fact that she spoke the same language didn't even register as strange at that time. I was conscious of only three things: that I was looking at a real life faerie, that she was as beautiful as one might expect, and, a little belatedly compared to the first two, that she was talking to me. I was able to muster "I'm glad to hear it" as a reply.

"Did you come through the portal?" she asked.

"The wormhole? Yes, I did."

"Incredible! I've never seen anything come through one yet." The faerie's voice began to speed up with excitement. "Tell me, what race are you? Where are you from? How do you create the portals? What -"

"Slow down." I said with a slight laugh.

The faerie chuckled. "Sorry. I get excited about the portals. My name is Anya."

"Wolfgang, though most just call me Wolf." I replied as I offered my hand. She looked at it curiously, and it took a moment for me to realize that handshakes may not be a known greeting to the faerie. "My people will shake hands when they meet. A gesture of trust."

"Interesting." Anya's eyes lit up as she gently took my hand. She started to say something else, then caught herself.

"What?" I asked.

"I just have so many questions, and the moment I ask one I'll ask a hundred. Will you go back through when the portal reopens? Ah, there I let one through." She laughed at herself. "I would love to pick your brain for a couple days, but I feel it is only polite to ask about your plans."

Fear gripped my heart again. "I don't know when the next test will be, or if it will even be successful. I wasn't supposed to be here."

Anya tilted her head in surprise. "Not supposed to... next test? And you don't know how it works?"

"I don't. My father is the director of the collider that generates the wormhole. He would know how it works, but the wormhole isn't forming where he wants it."

"You mean that it appears haphazard in your world as well?"

"Yea- wait, haphazard?"

Anya grinned. She must have found my sudden shift in thought funny. "Yes. It appears everywhere within a relative radius of about ten thousand metra from the spire in Bramblehome." she explained as she pointed to the city by the river. "I get plenty of exercise chasing it whenever I'm not in class."

"I take it that it's a unit of length, but what is a metra?"

I watched as Anya looked to the ground, then held her hand parallel to it at about her waist's height. "About there."

That's close to a meter back home. Easy enough. "How do you track the wormhole?"

Anya reached into her satchel and pulled out a tablet. "I found the porta-... sorry, wormhole, while I was flying to visit my family in Silverdew. That's where I'm from."

She stepped next to me to show what was being displayed. "Anyway, the next time it appeared in a meadow I was flying over. Everyone thought I was crazy when I told them about it, though the authorities did have concerns that it could explain some of the raiders attacks recently. I kept quiet about the por-, wormholes, after that and built a small sensor that could pick up on its unique frequencies. It has been opening more frequently as of late, and in multiple bursts. I suppose you would know about that?"

"I would." I replied, barely keeping up with her. "They have been able to run test sets in batches, trying to see what variables might bring the wormhole within the collider."

"Within it..." she touched her hand to her lips as she thought out loud. "That would mean that it isn't appearing where you'd expect, so the changing variables are causing the location of its appearance to move. That would seem to mean that it is tethered between our worlds specifically in these two locations." She glanced up at me. "I mean Bramblehome and wherever your collider is. When is the next test?"

"I told you, I don't know exactly when the next test will be."

"Ah, yes. Forgive me."

"However," I said with a raised palm to keep her from going off again, "that should have been the first test for today. I would expect at least three more over the next eight hours or so."

"Hours? A measure of time, yes?"

"We divide our day into twenty-four hours."

"Day being the time between your sunrises?" she asked.

"Yes." Had to give her this, the pretty faerie had quite the brain to her.

"Interesting division, though that would be from your planet's rotation that you have those numbers, correct?"

"I believe it's a holdover from the ancient Babylonians some four or five thousand years ago." Seeing that Anya didn't know the term, I explained "A year would be one orbit around our sun."

"That makes sense. What solar stage is your sun in?" She held up her hand, stopping herself. "Never mind, those terms are most likely to be radically different. Since you are stuck here until the next test, as you say, what do you plan to do?"

Now that the science fair was over, I could catch my breath. "Well, I wasn't really prepared to do anything. Though, if you could help me get back, I would be very grateful."

Anya tried to hide her disappointment. "That's understandable. I guess I can't just take you back with me, either. You have no wings to fly with and carrying you would cause a scene."

"Good observation." I jested.

Anya rolled her eyes, though her smile returned. "I can't very well hide you even if we got back. The university is in the middle of the city, and you'd be found out soon enough. Then we'd have a lot of questions asked of us that frankly I don't think we even know the answers to."

"I can agree with you there."

"Tell you what, I will try to get you to the next wormhole, but you need to promise me that you will find a way to come back."

"I definitely would like to." I said easily. I was finding Anya to be great company, and that innate curiosity to explore was starting to burn again.

"The only real issue would be getting you to fly." she interjected. "Then we could meet beyond where the wormholes are opening and be less likely to get caught."

"What would we be doing that would get us in trouble if we got caught?" There was an insinuation there that I only realized as I said it, and I tend to grin when embarrassed.

She caught both, and instead of recoiling at the thought she brought her hand back to her lips to try and hide a smile. This time she managed to stay quiet until her thoughts were finished. "I think we both would benefit from knowing each other more before we tried that."

"I didn't mean to imply it when I said it."

"I know. I could tell by the color of your face." she remarked. We both laughed at this. "So, how do we get you wings?"

It was a bit of a surprise that she stopped there instead of continuing, but it did allow me to remember what I was working on back home. "Believe it or not, I'm developing my own wingsuit at the research institute. The key problem has been the propulsion units, but I have also looked at getting some kind of neural connection engineered." He tapped his forehead as he said this, hoping that would help her understand the term.

Anya's eyes lit up again. "I can't do anything to help with your propulsion, but one of my professors is the head of thought-pattern engineering. If you can get the wings made, I can get the thought net figured out."

I just about leapt at the offer, but one thing held me back. "I would assume our brains are not wired the same. How would we control that?"

Her hand moved. "We would need to bring you in at that point or arrange for the suitable equipment to be moved to a hidden location." Then she waved her hand towards me.

I waited for her to say something, but several seconds went by in silence. "What was that for?"

Anya smiled. "I think that would do. Have a look." She flicked her hand up, and along its path a reflective mirror appeared. For a while I stood stunned. Not only did she understand plenty of science, but magic existed in her world as well.

The mirror was one thing, but the set of wings that now rested on my back were an entirely different matter.

"They are illusions." she said after a few moments. "You don't have the physical muscles to move them, but they will pass at a mere glance. I can get you in with that look, but never flying will draw attention to you."

Her tablet beeped. Anya's eyes instantly went to the screen. As she read, a gleeful smile broke across her face, and she pointed behind me. "The next wormhole is opening, about eight hundred and fifty metra in that direction."

There was something in that smile that didn't match her disappointment earlier when I mentioned leaving. "What's the smile for?"

I instinctively knew the look in her eyes. Mischief, curiosity's favorite cousin.

Anya pointed. "See those trees? There's a ravine behind them that's between us and the wormhole's frequency. You'll never reach it on foot, so the only way you'll be able to get there in time is if I carry you."

"Moving a bit fast, aren't we, Anya?"

She gave me a brilliant smile. "Well, it is the fastest way to get you there."

We shared a laugh, then I let her carry me. I could tell that it was some strain on her by the slight grimace on her face, but she flew without complaint.

Just as her tablet said, the wormhole was sitting right by the ravine's edge. We landed, and the wormhole was still open. How much longer I couldn't well risk. I turned to her and said, "I need to go through before it turns off."

"Will I see you again?"

I had been thinking of the answer during the flight. "Count on it." I then kept my eyes on her while I stepped through the wormhole. "Thanks for your help. I'll see you soon."

"Good luck." She replied.

I ended up in a different part of the caverns, but one that I managed to get out of.

I still haven't told anyone on this side of the wormhole about it.

*
**

Wolfgang looked at the document he'd finished typing. It was basically nothing more than a journal entry, a momentary reflection as he took a break from his parameter checks. The wingsuit was coming along, but he needed some specific help.

He smiled, then deleted the entire file. Looking down at his watch he began counting down the minutes.

Test in two hours, Anya.

"SURVIVAL GAMES"

Unsubmitted story for Contest #48.

Luke felt the breeze playing across his face and his bare arms. He dismissed it as he tried to stay asleep, then he bolted upright as he realized that a breeze that gentle shouldn't be inside the van.

Reality confirmed his initial conclusion. The moon was covered by thick bands of clouds, but some stars sparkled through their openings. Nearby he saw the still waters of a small lake, and all around were tall pine trees.

There was only one conclusion. They'd got him again.

I need to stop falling asleep in the van. Luke thought as he got to his feet. He reached into his pocket and pulled out his phone. The charge was only about five percent, and the bars showed he had no service.

"Just my luck." He powered off the phone and put it back in his pocket. The others must have decided to use his ill-advised nap to put him in another survival situation in the middle of the woods.

It was a game that he had joined at the start of the year, but had a long history. Being poor college students, they couldn't fly to the great locales of the world like several TV shows had started doing, but the wilderness near the college had enough thrill for a few days' worth of fun.

The others would stay close enough that they could help Luke if needed, and if he found either them or another person before the weekend was over, he would win.

This cadre of wilderness enthusiasts he'd found at college had operated unofficially for a decade, on three generations of peers if you weren't held back or graduated early. Though Cody and Kelsey were the senior ringleaders for his generation, he had swiftly risen among their ranks as the daring young freshman alongside Allison and Damien. One day he'd be the senior looking out for the next freshman generation.

He waited for that day with both excitement and regret; excitement at pulling the same stunts on the freshman he'd endured, and regret that his time would be at an end.

Luke focused his mind on the current scenario. A quick search revealed his pack lying beside a nearby tree and he hurried over to it. The old keepsake gave him hope. Coming back from a day at the beach, he was only equipped with his sandals, swim shorts, and a muscle shirt.

Nowhere near ideal clothing.

He investigated the pack and was pleasantly surprised to find that it hadn't been ransacked this time. His fire kit, water tablets, cloak, food rations, and sheathed bowie knife were all still there in the main slot. In the smaller pouch were his map, binoculars, and compass. The map was deceptively large and detailed, covering nearly two hundred miles from campus in any direction.

So far, they hadn't bothered to drive outside of that radius. Now all he needed to do was find a landmark and make his way home.

As he repacked, he couldn't help but think of one of the others being stuck out here instead of him. Their packs would possibly be far less prepared than his was, except for Allison of course. Her pack was even more thorough, and even then, she really didn't need any of it. Luke was convinced that Allison could survive anything and anywhere with her wits.

With the pack secured, he pulled the cloak around his shoulders and secured the sheath to his side with a length of rope. Luke knew that he must be quite the sight. They always took pictures when one of them got back.

Looking up, he tried to see through the trees. To the south and west was either flat land or a drop, for he could see nothing, but to the northeast he saw a decent hilltop that he could climb. Setting his feet and muttering a swift prayer, he started out.

Though he could see the rise as he weaved through the forest, his optimism began to fade. The forest floor had hardly any underbrush, far different from the pine forests around campus. The floor also immediately began to break into rolling gulleys with creeks sitting in their depths.

This was unlike any place he had been dropped in before, and he hoped that he could reach the top of the hill quickly to find his bearings.

Crossing the fifth or sixth creek, he paused. Though the night was cool, he still shouldn't be wandering through an unknown landscape at night. It wouldn't just be for fear of what was in the forest. If he wandered off while the others weren't looking, he'd lose their help if the need arose.

He needed to make camp for the night and rest, then he could make his way home in the morning. The night seemed eerily like that one those three summers ago.

Luke's hand instinctively moved to his left shoulder and the bite scars. It was still something of a miracle that his scrawny self had managed to kill the cougar that jumped him, stabbing repeatedly with his knife while the cat chewed towards his neck.

That should have ended his outdoors enjoyment, but he had found the near-death experience exhilarating. The feeling of acting against true terror, of knowing every action has a life-or-death result; very little could hope to frighten him afterwards.

As he looked around for a place to build a quick shelter, Luke noticed the faint glowing light of a fire to the northwest. Though it would take him away from the hilltop, fire generally meant civilization. His heart leaped. This would be the fastest survival run in history. After a prayer of thanks, he took off at a run.

As he came closer, he could see that there was more than one fire blazing, and soon he could hear the music of flutes and tambourines. This wasn't just a family camping; it seemed more like he'd stumbled into a family reunion in this remote corner of the world.

Nearer still his legs carried him. A myriad of voices reached him, singing and laughing. A horse whinnied into the night.

A horse?

Something hit him from behind and he fell sprawling to the ground. When he rolled over, two men stood over him. They were dressed in leather armor and held their spear points only a few inches from his neck.

"What are you doing here?" the one on the right asked him. Luke could just make a scar over his right eye.

Great, I've run into some hippie LARP session in the woods. Thanks guys. "I'm sorry," Luke began, letting some adrenaline-fueled fear escape in his voice, "I am lost and saw the fires."

"Where are you from?" the other asked. This man had a hooked nose, but little else was apparent in the moonlight.

"I'm from Kansas." Luke replied, not wanting to give more information.

"Never heard of it." the one with the hooked nose said and looked to the one with the scar over his eye. "You?"

"Me either. Might explain those strange clothes he's wearing." Scar replied after shaking his head.

Man, these guys are really in character.

"All right, get up." Hooknose ordered. Luke complied, hoping that at any moment they would stop acting. He smiled when he realized that he was almost a head taller than the two. Hooknose continued, though a little less sternly. "Go down to the encampment and ask for the commander."

Luke sighed. "Okay. What should I ask him for?"

The sarcasm was rewarded with a punch to the side of his head, quite a feat for Scar. "Don't talk back to us, boy! Just ask to speak with him."

"Alright, alright." Luke said as he got to his feet. "I'll go get him."

As Luke walked down towards the fires of the encampment, he began counting the number of tents and larger pavilions. There must have been a couple hundred people down there by the look of it. Five of the pavilion tents were beautifully adorned in red and silver cloth and formed a semicircle near the center of the camp. The whole setup looked quite impressive.

There were more soldiers down by the encampment. These ones wore metal plate armor and red mantle capes, looking more like what historical records depicted. A few near the edge of the camp saw him coming and turned to meet him. The one in the center had a crescent moon insignia pinning his cape to his shoulder. "Who goes there?"

"My name is Luke." He replied, thinking more and more about how silly he looked in his beach clothes and cloak compared to their attire.

"What are you doing here?"

"I was told to talk to your commander."

"Who told you?"

"The men on the hill."

"What m-" An arrow whipped past Luke's head and embedded itself in the leader's neck. Luke stared in horror as the man bled out in front of him. All around came shouts of terror and rage mixed with the clash of swords.

Luke hesitated for only a few more seconds before he ran into the camp. More arrows tore past him as he looked for somewhere to hide.

Another man rounded a pavilion that he was running towards. He held a large battleaxe and wore a long fur cape over his leather armor. The man reminded Luke of a Viking berserker. He saw Luke and started towards him with a look that Luke could only describe as murder in his eyes.

Fear gripped Luke, yet there was something else. Like against that cougar in the mountains, this was life-and-death. Just as that day, exhilaration filled his blood. He reached down and pulled the knife from his sheath. Then he turned and started running through the camp. The Viking followed.

Luke rounded the side of a tent, crouched out of view, and waited. At the first sign of the Viking, he silently lunged. His free hand gripped the battleaxe as the knife struck its blow.

The Viking coughed blood into Luke's face as his eyes slowly fell to see the knife penetrating his chest. The battleaxe landed with a thud next to them as the massive hands reached up as if to pull the blade out. Luke pulled the knife out himself before retreating out of the Viking's reach. Blood flowed freely to soak the ground beneath the man, and he fell dead to the earth.

Given time, Luke may have panicked at the sight of the man he'd killed. Instead, the sound of a girl's scream shattered his focus. Someone was in trouble.

Without thinking, he sheathed his knife and picked up the battleaxe before he rushed to help her.

He entered the pavilion just as three men finished their battle. The soldier with a red cape fell dead before two more in leather and fur. Behind the red cape were four girls in their nightgowns weeping in terror at the two men.

Luke was no longer reacting rationally, instead giving over to instinct and the latent, primal nature of battle. Without a word, he awkwardly swung the battleaxe and killed the man on the right with one blow, the axe head disappearing up to the shaft through the leather. Luke left the weapon in the man, drawing his knife and turned on the remaining combatant.

The second man started to strike, then stared aghast for a moment as he recognized Luke. The hesitation proved fatal as Luke jammed the knife home into Hooknose's throat. Luke stepped back and removed the knife, his hand bathed in blood as the man fell choking to his death.

Having made sure there were no other fur capes nearby, Luke took the sword from the hand of the first man. He then looked up at the girls.

The oldest of them was about the same age as he was, and the others had gathered behind her. She had radiant brown hair even in the dim torchlight, and her eyes were dark and lovely. Luke felt an instant attraction, just as when he'd first met Allison.

Both she and the others were terrified, as he would have imagined he would be in their place. Though the others looked at him with relief, she still looked at him with fear.

"Are you alright?" Luke asked, trying to calm them as he moved away from the entrance. Four more red capes and a half dozen furs littered the ground as he made his way to the girls.

Their leader nodded, stepping in front of the others as if to protect them. "Who are you?"

"My name is Luke. I was lost and wandered into your camp when the fighting began."

"Where are you from?" she asked.

"Kansas." he replied sarcastically. Again, she gave him that same confused look that the now-dead furs had on the hill. "Where are you from?"

"I am Princess Megan Starfall of Cyanna."

"Where is that?" Luke asked without thinking. He began to remind himself that these people were in character when it dawned on him that this couldn't possibly be a roleplaying session. Men were actively killing each other outside the pavilion.

He had killed...

The adrenaline and exhilaration that had fueled his actions fled as the weight of his actions fell on him. His heart raced and his vision began to blur, and then the sensation of falling as his legs gave way. The heat of the central fire was right beside his head when the sensation ceased. Megan's voice called out to him.

Or was it Allison's?

As he lay on his back struggling against unconsciousness, he caught the full might of the lunar light through the pavilion's smoke hole.

Three moons sat glowing in the heavens.

No way!

Then the darkness took hold.

AFTERWORD

Thank you again for reading this collection of tales from my earliest writing days.

If you have any feedback as to the stories within, please reach out to me. I am always looking to improve my craft, and I can't always see where I am weak.

Until next time, take care, and may God bless you in the days ahead.

www.ingramcontent.com/pod-product-compliance
Lightning Source LLC
Chambersburg PA
CBHW050330110726
47899CB00007B/2441